LUNAR AWAKENING

Saryssa VanBibber

Illustrations by: Mariana Costa
and Kimxasoto

Copyright

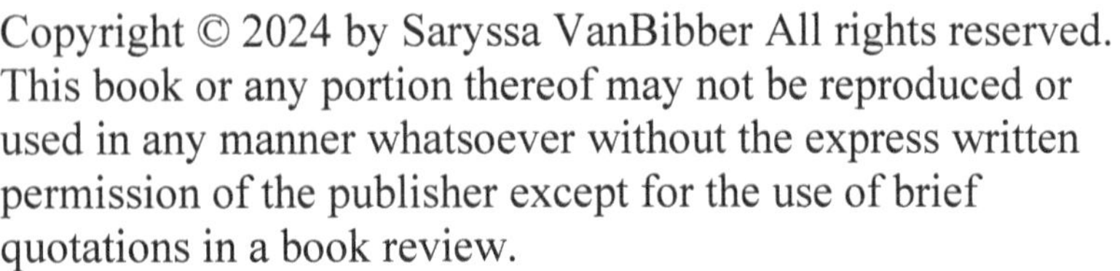

First Edition, 2024 ISBN: 979-8-9886040-6-8

EireneBros Publishing LLC 4414 82nd St, Ste 212, -318 Lubbock, TX 79424 www.eirenebrospublishing.com www.facebook.com/EireneBrosPublishing.

Table of Contents

Thanks

This book is dedicated to my mother, who helped cultivate my creativity and passion for writing. Thank you for helping me overcome my Dyslexia, for teaching me how to read and write, and for all those hours you spent reading to me. I will never forget your kindness and dedication to helping me succeed. I love you more than I say.

Thank you.

CONTENT WARNING:

The following contents contain depictions of violence, gore, and death and may contain sexual themes. Please use caution when reading.

1 Capital of Urufu
2 Mount Tsukismo
3 Capital of Turuk
4 Dunes of Orak
5 Capital of Tepli
6 Plains of Gruilo
7 Capital of Elrin
8 Orchards of Selren
9 Capital of Heltavin
10 Swamp of Woes
11 Dragons Spine
Continent of
5
7
4
6
11
9
10
2
3
1

Chapter One

Hard Beginnings

URUFU, A PEACEFUL country on the continent of Lud, a multicultural continent with vast terrain. Urufu is a country with the Dragon's Spine, where it is said that a giant, ancient dragon's skeleton is overgrown by nature to make mountains and valleys. The largest of the mountains is fabled to be the head of the dragon, called Mount Tsukismo. Urufu is in the middle of the continent and has a long, rich history of being the country that cultivates magic. The continent's greatest magical minds and practitioners usually come from Urufu. This blessing of magic is attributed to the Moon Goddess, one of the many gods the continent worships.

Urufu is widely known as a mostly pacifist country, firmly believing in peace, cooperation, and respect. This deep cultural belief is a primary code of their society, except for the continent's most aggressive neighbor, Heltavin. Heltavin is the continent's most military-minded country and home to its most strategic minds. Tales say that Heltavin's leaders were barren of magic and jealous of the Urufian people.

Other countries of Lud include the Elven nation of Elrin, which has bountiful trees that produce many fruits. The elves are great hunters and can track a man for days. The country of Tepli consists of boundless plains and is known for its agriculture. They are home to the largest men and women, most towering above the rest of the continent's population. And then there's the desert land of Turuk. There are tales that deep within the desert, an ancient castle has a crystal that allows the bearer to talk to the gods.

"Mommy, mommy! Look what I found!" Tsuki, the young princess of Urufu, called out as she ran towards her mother, standing in the inner garden with the young king's advisor, Takagi. She was running down a corridor to the green space with a very perturbed frog in her hands.

Kusay, Tsuki's mother, smiled and giggled as her daughter ran up to her with the angry amphibian, trying to wiggle free from Tsuki's tight grip on its body. Her long brown hair was pulled into a loose bun with golden accessories. Her dark skin glistened in the midday sun above. She was originally from the country of Turuk and an esteemed ambassador who happened to fall for the quirky young king of Urufu, who wooed her upon their meeting. "Sweetie, why don't we put him in the pond? That way, he has a place to stay."

"Excellent idea, Your Majesty," Takagi, the king's advisor and court wizard, stepped up and took the frog from Tsuki while handing his handkerchief to

Kusay so she could clean Tsuki's hands. Takagi wore a simple dark gray attire and his long blue hair in a ponytail. The young wizard was the apprentice of the former court wizard, who died a few years prior, leaving Takagi to learn as he went. Being only thirteen then, it was a huge shock when his mentor passed suddenly. Takagi did his best to honor his late mentor and do the job before him properly, but he made mistakes occasionally.

As Kusay cleaned her daughter's hands, she asked Tsuki, "And what do we say to those who help us?"

"Oh! Thank you, Takagi!" Tsuki cheered.

Kusay cleared her throat softly.

"I mean, Teacher." Tsuki corrected, speaking softer this time.

After cleaning his hands in the water, Takagi ruffled Tsuki's silver hair and said, "Thank you, little one."

Tsuki beamed up at the nickname he had given her.

After a moment of comfortable silence, a call came from one of the many corridors leading to the garden.

"My loves!" cried Tsuki's father. His grandparents named him Stephan. He continually surpassed everyone's expectations. He was a great leader.

“My liege!” Takagi said as he bowed.

Tsuki’s father laughed as he approached. “Rise, dear friend,” the king commented to Takagi. “I’m glad all of you are having a good afternoon.”

“Dad!” Tsuki exclaimed as she ran to her father. “I found a froggy!”

“Oh?” said Tsuki’s dad, chuckling. “My love,” he addressed his wife, “You are needed in the council room.”

“Shall I follow you?” asked Tsuki’s mother.

Her father nodded. He ruffled Tsuki’s hair and said, “Please stay with Takagi, my dear.”

She nodded as she knew her father and mother were essential and needed to go to the council who needed guidance.

“Daddy, have a good meeting!” she exclaimed, waving her parents goodbye.

Takagi cleared his throat as the two turned a corner, “Now, what shall we do?”

“Huh?” Tsuki questioned.

Takagi squatted to Tsuki's eye level. “We could have a history lesson or review the other countries.”

Tsuki groaned and put her head in her hands. “But that stuff is boring! It’s about to be my birthday; why can’t we have fun?”

Takagi chuckled, "My job is to teach and guide you. If I let you slack off too often, I wouldn't be doing my job."

Tsuki gave her mentor a skeptical look. "I'm five."

"Ah! Almost five. Now, where shall I begin?" Takagi said as he sat on the nearby bench.

"Ugh!" Tsuki moaned as she stomped over to the wizard.

"Oh, I know; since your fifth birthday is tomorrow, why don't we talk about spirit power and the ceremony," the young man said excitedly. "Now, if you remember from my previous lectures, the pure water that flows from Mount Tsukismo, which you are named after, has magical properties. It allows those descendants of the Moon Goddess to obtain and use power that matches the person using it. This power comes from the user's spirit."

"I already heard all this," Tsuki mumbled, but not softly enough for Takagi not to hear.

Takagi raised an eyebrow and continued, "This power manifests as an animal. For example, my spirit animal is a hawk. And because of this, I can use the attributes of my animal. I can use my spirit power to turn into a hawk, or I can have hawk-like sight, just to name a few."

"Tell me what the ceremony is like!" Tsuki burst out.

Takagi glared at the child next to him. Even though she was a royal, Tsuki was just like any other child her age. “Ahem.”

“Oh. can you tell me about the ceremony, please?” Tsuki asked softly.

Takagi gave a pleased smile and nodded, “The ceremony has the child being anointed at the edge of the water that flows directly from Mount Tsukismo. An esteemed elder tells the child to go into the water up to their chest and look into it. Then, the child will see an animal. Of course, the elder will see it too, so there is no mistake about what animal the child's spirit power is. And that’s it! The child will come out of the water and dry off while the elder announces the animal. Then we feast!”

Tsuki jumped up and yelled, “Food! Yay!”

The very next day was the young princess’s fifth birthday. Tsuki’s special day was supposed to be perfect. The fifth year of a Urufian’s life was when they found their Spirit Power, a cause for celebration. But what unfolded was no less than a tragedy.

As the young king and queen guided Tsuki through the forest to the choosing waters, events rapidly unfolded that toppled her world. Her father was the youngest of two boys. He had passed his older brother for the throne because of his prowess in strategy and fighting. Her mother was a diplomat from a foreign land at peace with Tsuki's.

Tsuki's father wore his customary military outfit. He had a deep blue jacket with golden shoulder pads and tassels. Tsuki always loved playing with those and the many medals her father wore on his chest. Even though he was only in his mid-thirties, her father had hints of gray hair in his usual black. This was because of the demanding duties of being a good king. He also sported a bushy mustache. His eyes were thinner than her mother's but just like Tsuki's.

Tsuki had silver hair that fell a little past her shoulders. She had slitted eyes like her father, but they were light blue. She was a bit pudgy and short for a five-year-old, but she was nonetheless healthy. Her light olive skin glowed in any light. She wore a white dress with short sleeves that reached her shins. She also wore white sandals and a crown of daisies on her head.

As they walked, her parents discussed whether she would take after them or have a different path. Tsuki looked at her father to ask a question and saw a feather falling from the sky. As it floated toward the ground, Tsuki bumped into her father's arm. It was an abrupt stop, which startled her.

Looking forward, Tsuki saw a man dressed in black holding a very long blade, longer than her father's, which he always kept by his side. It was the sword of the king, after all.

"Daddy?" Tsuki whispered as she stared at the man in black.

"Stay back, sweetheart," her father commanded.

Suddenly, the man started towards the three at a brisk pace.

Tsuki's father pulled his sword, but not quickly enough. He was run through by the man's blade, blood spraying Tsuki as she took cover behind her father. At first, she thought it was raining, but it was too warm. Then, she saw blood dripping from the tip of the sword embedded in her father.

Her mother screamed while her father dropped his own blade. Her mother rushed the man, holding a knife in her hands. The man pulled his sword from his first target and swung it at Tsuki's mother.

The next thing Tsuki saw was her mother standing there, with no head on her shoulders and blood spraying everywhere. Tsuki stumbled backward and fell. She looked at her feet only to find her mother's head looking at her. Tsuki tried to scream, but nothing came out.

Then the man in black pulled back his hood and stared at Tsuki, tears in his green eyes.

"I don't want to kill you. But if I don't, he'll kill my family," the man said as he slowly walked towards the frail little girl. As he came closer, Tsuki saw a purple snake head on his hand that was holding his sword. Tsuki felt something in the grass and grabbed it out of reflex. It was her father's sword. She barely blocked the killing blow; it deflected off. The man's sword cut deep into the flesh vertically on Tsuki's left eye. The wound was wide and long and gushed blood.

Tsuki then scrambled away, trying to get into the trees that surrounded the path, but not before the man swung twice, cutting deep within the flesh on her back.

"I'm going to kill you, so there's no use in running," the man said as he lunged again.

The whole world seemed to freeze, silent and still. Suddenly, a force awakened within Tsuki. A power she did not know she had. She closed her eyes because it hurt. Something burst forth from the cuts on her back, and she felt them move; it was warm. Instinctively, she moved them and was quickly lifted off the ground. As she opened her eyes, expecting to feel the cutting of a blade in her, she found that she was above the man. She was flying! Tsuki looked around her, expecting to find someone above with a guardian who could fly, but all she saw were wings. One of a dove and the other of a bat.

She didn't know what had happened, but as she looked down at the now enraged man, she didn't care. All she knew was that she could get away.

So, with her father's sword in hand, Tsuki took off in a random direction and flew as far as she could to get away, wondering if the man could fly by magic or not.

She flew for quite some time until her body gave out. She had been existing on pure fear and adrenaline, and when that gave out, she fell from the sky. Thankfully, several trees broke her fall.

When Tsuki awoke, she expected it all to have been a bad dream. She thought she would wake up on her fifth birthday, and her mother and father would be beside her. Instead, she could see the inside of a dim, dank hut made of straw and wood. She was in tremendous pain, and that's how she knew it wasn't a dream.

"Ah, you're awake," said a man from across the hut.

She knew it wasn't the man who had attacked her or her parents because his voice was different. It was deeper and smoother.

"How do you feel?" the man asked.

"I hurt," Tsuki said with tears in her eyes. Even though she was very grownup for her age, she still reverted to simple things like crying when injured.

"I know. I'm sorry," he cooed soothingly.

Tsuki then looked down to see a bite mark on her wrist. She didn't remember what happened in the incident with the dark figure. She looked questioningly at the man who was at her side.

"To save you, I had to turn you into one of my kind, a werewolf. You would have died if I hadn’t given you rapid healing abilities. It seems to have had an adverse effect on you," the man said softly.

"A were-what?" Tsuki asked as she tried to sit up. Her throat was dry; she needed water. When she realized she could not, she lay back down and motioned to the man that she needed water.

"Oh, yes, of course." He eagerly stood up from his chair and walked to a table.

Now Tsuki could see that the man was tall, like a tree. He had dark brown hair with strange dog ears and a flowing tail to match the color of the hair on his head. The man also had a big, full beard and mustache that he kept running his hand through. He wore a red shirt that was open at the front. He also had hair on his chest, just like Tsuki's father. From what Tsuki saw, he was also barefoot.

He was just like the werewolves in her mom's stories: hairy all over, with an imposing aura, wolf ears on his head, and a fluffy tail.

He brought over a wooden cup and helped Tsuki drink from it.

As she finished drinking, Tsuki asked, "Where am I? And where are my parents?"

The man breathed deeply and said, "You're in my home deep within the great Urufian forest. I don't know where your parents are. You fell from the sky and crashed into a lot of trees. My son Kiriuk found you. After I turned you, I helped heal your wounds. They may take some time to fully heal, though."

Then, Tsuki saw a little boy around her age with silver hair, wolf ears, and a tail to match.

"So it really happened?" Tsuki said as she began to cry again.

"What happened, little one?" the man asked.

Tsuki then recounted the horrific tale to the man. She wished the story was not true and had just been a nightmare. But it wasn't a dream. It was real, and she had to face that fact when she told the man what had happened.

"And all of that happened yesterday? My word," said the werewolf man. "No wonder you were so close to death. I'm glad we found you."

The little boy named Kiriuk now stood at his side, hesitant to speak as he was timid.

"You were really hurt. I'm glad you're with us now," Kiriuk said as he tentatively walked forward.

And that was the start of a new life for Tsuki. She spent seven years with them, learning to hunt and control her new werewolf powers. At the time, Tsuki thought about the wings she had grown but soon forgot about them as she focused on mastering her werewolf powers.

Chapter Two

It All Burns

TSUKI HAD BEEN living with the werewolf man, who said his name was difficult and to call him Alpha and Kiriuk for a few weeks as she healed. She learned that Kiriuk was actually a wolf that had been cursed to become a boy. Alpha was a lone werewolf, which was strange as they usually lived in groups called packs.

Alpha was very kind to ensure she was happy and fed; he even played a few games with her. He even had some wooden toys that she and Kiriuk played with. He wasn't the greatest cook and nowhere near the castle cooks back home, but Tsuki ate what was given to her as she knew it was there to help her get stronger.

Soon, she was healed enough to learn how to use her werewolf powers. Alpha taught her that she was faster and stronger than an average human. He had her run laps around the clearing and punch stones in a nearby cave.

A few months passed, and she began to figure out how to control these aspects of her new self. Then, Alpha taught her about transforming into her true self. It was complicated and strange, and it hurt too. Tsuki had a difficult time with the process of transforming into a full werewolf. She would attempt to fully transform but only convert a portion of her body.

After weeks that felt like months, Tsuki fully transformed. In her transmuted state, she stood only about 5 feet tall. Her fur was light grey, almost the silver color of her hair. Under her fur, she had more defined muscles than a typical child.

"Wonderful," Alpha said, clapping his hands. " Continue to focus on pushing out. After a while, you will get used to the feeling and can stay like this for extended periods."

Tsuki looked around and saw a world full of extremely bright colors. It was as if the brightness of daylight was higher than it had been before. She also took a breath through her nose. As she did so, a whirlwind of scent filled her nostrils and almost became too much to bear.

Quickly returning to her original state, Tsuki fell to the ground with an "Oof!"

"Well done, Tsuki. That's enough for today. We will work on making the process easier and more natural for you," Alpha praised as he helped Tsuki off the ground.

"Now you can play with me!" Kiriuk shouted as he ran up to Tsuki.

Tsuki sighed. Kiriuk was always much more energetic than she was, and after transforming, she was slightly tired.

Kiriuk stared at the older girl with his best sad puppy face, making his bottom lip quiver, "Please, Tsuki?"

Tsuki hung her head, "Give me 5 minutes, and then we can play hunter and prey. But I get to be prey this time!"

Kiriuk jumped up joyfully, "Deal!" he ran into the cabin. He returned with a wooden cup of water, hoping the drink would make Tsuki want to play faster.

Years passed, and Tsuki felt the two males were like family to her, even calling Kiriuk brother. The two became very close, even making their own calls for hunting together.

One day, while hunting with Kiriuk, Tsuki smelled something odd while walking back to the cabin. She couldn't recognize the odor.

Then Kiriuk yelled out, "Smoke!"

Once they realized that something was off, they broke out into a run toward the cabin. In the clearing, a roaring fire had engulfed the cabin.

"No! Father!" Kiriuk screamed as he ran into the burning structure.

Tsuki followed behind, tears streaming down her face. As she burst into the house, she saw Kiriuk knelt beside Alpha. The man had been run through by several spears, six in total. One of the spears was obviously in one of his lungs. His blood soaked into his tunic made from a sack. His head was hung low, eyes glassy. Tsuki was afraid he was already dead.

"Kids!" cried the werewolf when he saw the two and immediately coughed, blood spewing everywhere, running down his chin. "Oh, thank the Gods… You need to listen to me. I need you to run. They will be back soon," the man gasped in a hoarse voice, blood spilling out of his mouth with every word. It appeared to Tsuki that he was close to death because of the amount of blood on the ground surrounding him.

"No, we can't leave you here!" Kiriuk protested.

Tsuki had always been the more mature of the two, whether from her upbringing or trauma. It didn't matter now. All she knew was they had to get out of there. So Tsuki grabbed her father's sword, grabbed her brother by the collar, and dragged him out of the burning cabin. Kiriuk was kicking and screaming between coughs as he was dragged out. He kept repeating how they couldn't leave Alpha there like that.

As she passed through the doorway, she heard Alpha say weakly, "Good girl."

Once Tsuki had slapped sense into her brother after a fight, they ran with Kiriuk leading. He had always been the better hunter and knew the woods better than anyone. But as they ran, Tsuki fell behind and lost sight of her brother.

"Kiriuk, wait up!" she called ahead. There was no answer. She then came to a fork in the hunting path that they were taking. There was no sign of Kiriuk.

"Which way did he go?" Tsuki wondered out loud. She took the left road and soon came upon a village. "Maybe I can wait here and then return to the cabin to find Kiriuk."

It was then that her fate took another wrong turn. As she ran, Tsuki stepped into a noose trap on the ground. The rope now wrapped around her foot lifted her in the air, hanging her upside down.

"Well, well, well. Look here, boys. Caught ourselves a pup," said a grimy-looking man who came out of the trees. He and his compatriots were holding large knives and clubs.

Tsuki flailed around, trying to get free. As the men approached her, she struggled, making it hard for them to get close. Suddenly, Tsuki's arms were grabbed from behind, but not before she sliced into the assailant with her claws she had learned to grow from her transformation.

"Ack!" cried the man who had grabbed Tsuki's arms.

“Hey! Remember not to damage the goods. That doctor guy likes clean subjects,” yelled another.

Tsuki struggled and nearly had the large man's grip off of her when more came to his aid. They then tied her up with a chain and gagged her, covering her head with a thick sack so she couldn't see. No matter how hard she tried, she couldn't escape, and they threw her into a wagon. As the wagon bumped along the rough road, she kicked and struggled on her binds, and she ended up connecting with the back of one of the men, nearly sending him tumbling off the cart.

"Ouch! Hey, someone get control of her. Knock her out or something."

It was then that Tsuki was hit on the head and blacked out.

When she awoke, she was in an almost pitch-black cell with nothing but a hole in the corner and a dirt floor. She immediately sprang to her feet and struggled against the bars of the cell.

"You can't get out," said someone across the way from her. Then, she noticed big yellow eyes and a small, frail boy who looked starving.

"What?" Tsuki replied.

"They are taking children and doing horrible things to them. They don't come back the same as when they left. If they come back at all," whispered the frail boy.

Suddenly, there was a loud creak of a metal door and a loud bang.

"Dr. Gruten, this is the one the men told us about. She's a fighter. Maybe she can stand the procedure," a man said as he came into sight.

"I am a werewolf; you can't defeat me! I am like the man who taught me to fight, strong and proud!" Tsuki yelled.

Another man chuckled as he came down the hallway. His voice was sharp and had an aristocratic air to it. "A fighter, hmm? And a werewolf. We've never had one of those before. This should be interesting."

This man, who Tsuki guessed was Dr. Gruten, reeked of a horrible aroma that Tsuki could not describe, making her nose wrinkle. He wore all white with a black tie and black gloves that came to his elbows. He had blonde hair from what Tsuki could see in the darkness; it was short but puffed up in the front and flowed back. Something made Tsuki uneasy about his presence. Maybe it was his unsettlingly wide smile. But she didn’t have long to ponder this.

He knelt inches away from the bars as he was about to speak. Tsuki took the chance to swing at Dr. Gruten with her claws, making sweet contact. She had scratched him with her claws, blood spraying out in an intense burst, coating the ground.

"Gaaaah!" Dr. Gruten screamed as he fell backward. After checking his wound by touching his gloved hand to his face, he said, "Take her to the surgery room. And make sure she's secure. She'll pay for that!" he then got up and trounced off.

The next thing Tsuki knew, she was being grabbed by several men and taken into this pure white room. It smelled heavily of metal and had a sharp scent that burnt her nose hairs.

"What are you going to do with me? What are you-?" Tsuki started to say, but a hard slap cut him off.

"Quiet, or I'll do it again," said one of the goons.

They quickly tied her to the metal slab in the center of the room and left, leaving her alone to stare up at the ceiling. She had several straps on her arms and legs: one across her shoulders, one around her neck, and one across her forehead. She could only move her hands, feet, and eyes.

Then, she saw Dr. Gruten burst into the room with several other men. He had a blood-soaked bandage across his cheek. This made Tsuki smirk.

"Tear her shirt off and prepare her for the operation," demanded Dr. Gruten to the number of assistants in white lab coats like his.

"Do what?" Tsuki shouted as she began to struggle again, not making much progress but rubbing her skin raw from the restraints.

"And gag her too. I don't want to be disturbed while I work," Dr. Gruten said coldly behind the medical mask he was now wearing.

As they gagged her, Tsuki tried to bite but failed. She was now helpless against whatever the doctor was going to do to her.

After things settled, Dr. Gruten picked up a scalpel from a tray next to the metal slab. "Shall we begin?" Dr. Gruten said, his smile evident in his voice.

The next thing Tsuki knew was the slicing pain of the doctor cutting into her flesh. He cut from her sternum down to her belly in one smooth motion. Tsuki screamed around her gag, the pain overwhelming. The cut was deep, as far as she could tell. The doctor then brought his hand gripping the scalpel back up to her sternum. After that, it was a blur of pain until she passed out.

Chapter Three

Locked Inside

TSUKI WOKE IN a baggy shirt, lying on the dirt floor in her cell. Her body hurt so badly she could barely breathe. She forced herself to lift her head and saw stitches where Dr. Gruten had cut her. She looked across the way to see if the frail boy was there, but all she saw was an empty cell. Then Tsuki heard the metal door swing open. Her body tensed, and she played dead. Or, she tried, but the pain of the incision made it hard to breathe steadily.

Tsuki saw a plate of food with bugs crawling all over it. It reminded her of the time the Alpha killed a cockroach in the cabin in the first few days of her staying with him.

"There she is, still alive, huh," said one man. "Let's grab her. We can't keep the doctor waiting too long."

Tsuki noticed there were several men as they opened the door. They rushed in and grabbed her.

As they entered the white room, one man said, "Don't forget to take off her shirt this time. I had an earful from the doctor about the last patient. "

They then removed Tsuki's baggy shirt, making her feel cold. As they restrained and gagged her, one man gripped her ankles hard. She struggled at the touch, knowing nothing good would come out. They picked her up, taking her through the metal doors that led to that white room.

"Look at her squirm when I hold her," said the man as he continued to hold her down after they placed her on the slab.

"Quit it. You know the doctor prohibits touching the patients like that. It makes them tear open their wounds," said another.

"Oh, alright. Fine," said the first man.

As they left, Tsuki gave a shiver. Not because she was cold but because of the touch.

When the doctor came in with his assistants, he smiled. "Ah, your werewolf blood has made you heal faster than normal beings would. Perfect!" Dr. Gruten said as he ran a finger along the incision.

"My hypothesis is that the healing effect of her blood will keep her alive throughout the trial of the serum," said one of the assistants.

"Yes, I thought of that as well," said the doctor. He then took a syringe filled with a dark green liquid from the tray beside Tsuki. "Now we begin the real test," he said as he injected Tsuki with the green liquid. It felt like fire in her veins. It was just as bad as the incision. She thrashed at the pain.

As Tsuki flailed against her restraints, she shouted behind the gag, “What did you do to me? What is that stuff?”

“I have no obligation to explain anything to a test subject. But if you must know, it is a serum I developed over years of hard work,” Gruten stated matter-of-factly as he walked over to one of the other men in the room and wrote something down. Mumbling to himself, “Her left eye changed to silver.”

Gruten then turned back to her. “The ultimate, mindless, healing soldier. It enhances the body's healing processes and makes them easier to control.”

Tsuki’s eyes widened. Was he planning on selling this soldier to a country to help them fight a war? Was she going to become a mindless soldier? What exactly was he planning?

“Now,” the doctor continued, “we will let that take effect as we try cutting again. Hopefully, it will work so we can be recognized by the new king!"

There was a murmur of agreement from the assistants as Dr. Gruten started snipping the sutures off of Tsuki's stomach and chest. Then he started cutting with his scalpel again in the same spot as before, sinking in easier. Relief came when Tsuki passed out anew.

This became routine for Tsuki. She'd wake up as the brutes dragged her from her cell and handled her, exposed. Then, she was cut open again and occasionally beaten here and there. This seemed to have lasted for years. Tsuki couldn't keep up with time, so she didn't know how long it had been, but her body seemed to have matured, and her hair grew long. She had been broken, body and mind, and she didn't really care about staying alive anymore. The only salvation she had was thinking of her parents.

Then, one day, an assistant who was beating her let slip a secret as he was talking with another man outside the cell. "You know that there are rumors that the new king murdered the previous king and his family."

"Shhh. Do you want us to get caught? Keep quiet. And remember to keep her healthy for the doctor; he can tell if we've been beating her or not," said the other man.

"Right, right. I know," replied the first man.

Weeks passed, and this news repeated in Tsuki's head. "The man who killed my parents is the new king?" She said to herself. Was that the truth?

She didn't know what to think and wanted to figure out who it was. She was about to question it further, but the door squeaking interrupted her train of thought.

"Congrats! You're sixteen, according to what we've forced you to tell us. That makes you a woman now. How exciting for you!" said Dr. Gruten, clapping in front of her cell.

Tsuki didn't even move to look at him.

"Hmpf. Now, what's with the attitude, my dear? This is a momentous occasion! I will be finishing my examinations today, and then comes the brainwashing," he said as he opened the cell door and closed it behind him. Suddenly, one of the assistants burst in.

"Doctor! Doctor! The king sent us a letter! He will be here in three days to see our specimen!" The assistant said excitedly.

"Let me see that!" said the doctor as he stormed out of the cell, locking it behind him.

Tsuki was left alone for a few days, but the brutes suddenly came for her again.

"King Lentus will be here in a few hours. Let's get her ready," said one of the brutes.

The name Lentus rang in Tsuki's head. That was the name of her uncle. Was her uncle the king? Was he the one who ordered that man to kill her parents? She had to know.

"Now, newbie, you have to make sure you tie the restraints correctly, okay?" said one of the goons.

"R-right!" said the young man.

This time, as they restrained her, Tsuki felt her left arm was looser than usual. This was the arm the new man had tied. She thought, " This might be my way out. "

She stayed still, as she had done numerous times before, but it wasn't because she lacked strength this time. It concealed the fact that she could slip out of the restraints.

Once they left, Tsuki tugged on the restraint on her wrist. Once she freed her left hand, she deftly got out of the other restraints and stood independently for the first time in years. Tsuki felt her weight shifting as she took a few steps forward, her knees buckling a few times. She stumbled a bit but soon got her legs under her. She moved the rest of her limbs and stretched. Tsuki wasn't sure if she could escape, but she had to try.

Then, the only metal doors to the room opened. The young man had come back to check his work. Tsuki panicked, brought out her werewolf claws, and slashed the young man's chest. Blood sprayed the white walls with crimson and splattered across Tsuki's face. As he fell back, she felt the power within her return, just like it had come upon her when her parents died. It was a warmth where there once was an aching cold.

She felt like killing all of them. Every last one of the men in this horrific place. As Tsuki took a walk down the corridor, she knew killing these men would be against her parents' wishes. So, Tsuki attacked the goons and assistants without actually killing them. She did break several bones and maim everyone she came in contact with, though. She was getting them back for all that they had done to her. Her left eye was pure silver, and her right eye was blue. Her wings had grown out of her back. She had also transformed into a werewolf for the first time since she had been injected with that green goop.

She stopped in front of a door that read:

DR. QUELTMIUS GRUTEN.

She slowly opened the door with blood dripping off of her. Only when she stepped into the open doorway did the doctor look up.

"You know to knock before enteri- You! How did you get out?" Dr. Gruten said as he stood, shaking as he retreated against the wall. Tsuki noticed a familiar weapon propped against that wall.

"Tell me one thing, doctor. Who is the king?" Tsuki said through clenched teeth.

"It-it's King Lentus! The older brother of the previous king!" Dr. Gruten said in a panic.

"My uncle is the king, huh? I'll have to pay him a visit when I'm stronger." Tsuki said as she took steps toward the doctor.

"Wait, uncle? You're the-?" Dr. Gruten didn't get to finish his sentence before Tsuki clamped a hand around the doctor's mouth and crushed his jaw, making him pass out.

"I need to be stronger before I confront my uncle," she said as she took her father's sword from the wall behind the doctor's desk. Looking at the evil man's desk, Tsuki found papers describing the experiments that were going on in the compound.

A few years ago, King Lentus ordered Gruten to make soldiers with increased abilities who would follow through on any order made by a handler. Gruten used the serum to make these soldiers, which Tsuki was subjected to. Tsuki found nothing while she was searching for his motivation to do these awful things.

Chapter Four

A Better Life

BEFORE TSUKI STUMBLED out of the compound, she knocked a few more men to the ground and found where they ate. She then showered, changed clothes, and packed food for the journey ahead- which would be a long one.

Once outside, Tsuki retracted her werewolf form. She also admired her wings; the dove feathers were soft, and the batwing was smooth. Her wings then retracted into her back on their own. It was a strange and foreign feeling, but not uncomfortable.

Tsuki wore the only clothes she had found in the compound: a potato sack with holes. Her silver hair had grown to the middle of her back and flowed in the wind. She was about five feet tall as she stretched her limbs and sighed. She hadn't been able to do that in years, as her cage had gotten too small for her. She took a deep breath as she faced forward and started to walk.

As she walked, she came across a traveling merchant who told her she was in the country of Heltavin, the land of the vampires. The date he shared meant it was a few days after her sixteenth birthday.

She traveled to a small town in the shadow of a large castle that belonged to a count, which she found by asking around. As she walked through this town, she was stopped by a little old lady. The lady looked tired but all the more kind. This lady took Tsuki in after seeing her walk around in a sack and let her stay with her and another girl whom this lady had already taken in, Willianna. She was three years older than Tsuki and a few inches taller.

Willianna had short, dark brown hair and a mischievous smile. She usually walked around barefoot, as is the custom in the beach cities of the continent. Her clothing immediately marked her as a southern beacher, a person who lived on the south side of the continent. She wore a tan tube top with a golden sun and a dark blue skirt with one side hiked up. She was also a known marksman in the town with her slingshot that could easily crack bones.

It wasn't long until the two girls were inseparable, with chaos in their wake wherever they went. They were both mischievous at heart but never wanted people hurt, so they would pull harmless yet elaborate pranks on the townspeople. Tsuki would always get caught and have to apologize, ultimately landing her in a cell at the local sheriff's office. It wasn't long before she was out, whether she did her time or Willianna broke her out with her deft hands and lock-picking kit. The girls also had a habit of helping those in the town center where the market was, lifting things, mending boxes and structures, and carrying supplies.

Willianna also taught Tsuki some valuable skills like climbing and sneaking. They were climbing trees the sheer sid\.,m ne of the nearby mountain and even the side clock tower. Their favorite thing to do was sneak up behind the town guards and surprise them. The two got in a lot of trouble for trying to climb the castle of the count. They were spotted by the stable boy, who began to yell at them to get down. The girls immediately climbed down and ran to the old lady's house. Unbeknownst to the two, they had attracted the attention of the count.

Two years flew by, and sadly, the old lady passed, her kind heart giving out. She left Willianna the house and everything in it. And so the two girls lived in that house from then on.

One day, it was nearly eleven at night in the one-story house Tsuki shared with Willianna. She was talking with Willianna about mundane things and how bored she was.

“Tsuki, why don’t you want to go to the ball? It’ll be fun. You might even find yourself someone special,” Willianna begged Tsuki.

Tsuki scoffed, “Because I hate parties. Everyone just stares at me.”

Willianna sighed. “That’s because you’re so beautiful. Tsuki, come on! I can’t go by myself. What if I get kidnapped?”

“Well, you won’t get kidnapped. And if you do, I expect you to be back before supper,” Tsuki laughed.

Then suddenly, there was a knock at the door.

"Who would be knocking at this hour?" Tsuki got up to answer it. An old man around 60 years old stood there.

"Good evening, madam. I am Halt, the butler of Count Valin. He sends you this." Halt, a pale man with a very round dome, pointy chin, and goatee, gave Tsuki a letter. "My lord asks that you give the contents some thought, " Halt said, bowing. "Good night, madam." Then, with another slight bow, Halt left.

As he left, Tsuki saw he was skinny underneath his white shirt and black waistcoat. The waistcoat trailed down in the back, nearly scraping the ground as he rounded the corner.

Tsuki was shocked and confused. "What was that all about? I wonder what this is?" Tsuki closed the door, looking at the unopened letter.

Willianna walked over to Tsuki. "So… what does it say?"

Tsuki opened the letter. It said:

Dear Lady Tsuki.

I am the Count Alistain Valin. The annual ball is tomorrow. I know you do not have an escort, and I would be delighted to escort you. I will wait outside the Grand Hall, anticipating your agreement to attend. You'll know me when you see me.

Forever yours,

The Count

Willianna was jumping for joy. "Do you know who he is, Tsuki?"

"No, and I don't care," Tsuki said, crumpling the letter and throwing it on the floor.

Not paying attention to Tsuki's answer, Willianna picked up the paper. "The Count's the most handsome man in all of the land! He's charming and interesting… Why won't you go with him? You'll have fun. You need to live your life and not be locked up here forever. Please, Tsuki."

Tsuki sighs. "Fine, I'll go with him. But if things get weird, you'd better get me out of there. Got it?"

Willianna's smile grew wider. "Got it!" She launched herself to hug Tsuki. The girls sat up for some time chatting about things girls going to a party chat about: hair, clothes, makeup, and guys.

The next afternoon, Tsuki got up and started getting ready. "I can't believe I got talked into doing this," she said as she put on makeup.

"Because you're my best friend ever. And you are interested in what will happen," said Willianna, also putting makeup on.

Tsuki shook her head. "Yes, to the first part, no to the second."

Willianna hugged her friend, "You know you're excited." Then, there was a knock at the door.

"Ugh! What now?" Tsuki said as she answered the door. And there was Halt.

He was holding a dark blue and silver dress. He bowed. "Hello again, madam. My master has asked me to give you these." He handed her the dress and a silver mask with blue spikes on the sides. "Have a wonderful evening." he bowed and left.

Halt's quick and stiff bow reminded Tsuki of her father's advisor and the court wizard, Takagi. Tsuki always looked up to Takagi with curiosity as he appeared to have always defended her father in arguments.

But she had no time to think about her friend now. All she could think about was the beautiful dress. It was magnificent. It was a classic ball gown made of satin and silk. It even had a few gems on it. The main portion of the dress was a dark blue trimmed with silver, and it had a deep v-cut in the front. It also had leg-of-mutton sleeves that were silver and had blue trim.

Willianna closed the door. And at the same time, they both exclaimed, "Wow!" while they looked at the dress.

"Ok, now I have to go if he spent this kind of money on me!" Tsuki said as she stared at the dress.

They dressed quickly, eager to get to the ball at the Grand Hall near Tsuki's home. Tsuki wore the beautiful, stunning blue dress, and Willianna wore a dark green dress that balanced her bright blue eyes.

When they arrived, Willianna asked, "Do you want me to wait until you find him, or…"

"No, no, you go on ahead, I'll find you inside," Tsuki said, still looking for the Count.

"Ok then. Be careful," Willianna said as she left her friend to search.

Tsuki looked and looked for the Count but couldn't find him near the entrance of the Hall. Then, out of the corner of her eye, she spotted a man. He was tall, with sleek, long, black hair. He was wearing a dark red shirt and cloak, black pants, a red tie, with a red mask trimmed with black. Like Willianna said, he was very handsome. He watched Tsuki intensely with a half-evil, half-wanton smile.

She nervously walked up to him. Her heart was beating with anticipation. “Count?” she asked him.

"Correct you are, my beautiful rose,” Alistain said in a deep, sensual voice as he grabbed her hand and kissed it gently. His lips were soft like silk yet cold like ice. He then led her into the hall where the party was.

It was a very tall, expansive building made of marble and stone. Tables lined the hall's outside edge, leaving the center for the dance area.

The entire time they walked, Alistain kept his eyes on Tsuki, never leaving her face for an instant.

“You look stunning in that dress,” he said, leading her to a table at the back.

"Well, you're the one who picked it out for me." Tsuki smiled at him. She looked into his eyes. They were deep red, the color of his shirt. She found herself lost in them. His eyes were enticing, with a little hint of humor in them.

As the ball began, Alistain asked Tsuki to dance. They got up and walked to the dance floor. When the music started, Alistain put his right hand on Tsuki's waist and grabbed her right hand in his left. She placed her left hand on his shoulder. As they started to dance, Tsuki could feel his eyes on her, making her blush softly.

"You are even more gorgeous in person. The candlelight is making you glow even more than you already do," the Count said softly but loud enough that Tsuki could hear it.

Tsuki's wolf ears twitched at the compliment as blood rushed to her cheeks. "Th-thank you."

"Only speaking the truth," Alistain chuckled, "I was captivated by you ever since that evening you decided to climb my castle. I'll have to remember to give that stable boy a raise."

"Wait, that's what made you find me?" Tsuki asked, surprised.

Alistain laughed sharply, showing his fangs, "Yes, my dear. That is what brought our paths together. When he told me two girls were climbing the side of the castle wall, I had Halt take the boy and me to the town center, and the boy pointed you and your friend out. When my eyes laid upon your silver hair and soft yet fierce features, I was struck with infatuation. But, I heard you laugh, and like that, I was smitten," he looked at Tsuki lovingly.

"You fell in love at first sight?!" Tsuki exclaimed loudly, making many look at the two.

Chuckling, "I wasn't sure it was love, so I stole glances from afar, always watching, never touching," he said as he let his eyes wander down Tsuki's form, making Tsuki blush even more.

They continued talking until the end of the ball. Most of the attendants were either gone or at tables. Suddenly, Alistain pulled Tsuki close to him, their bodies touching.

"Tsuki, let us leave this place and go to my castle," Alistain said as he led her outside.

Tsuki tentatively smiled and nodded. She felt safe with this man, like he would protect her until the end. It was a nice feeling.

Outside, there was a carriage waiting for them. Willianna was also out front, looking for Tsuki. The friends locked eyes, and Willianna immediately tilted her head and gave a thumbs up, which Tsuki returned with a smile. Halt opened the door for his master and Tsuki, and they climbed in. Alistain sat across from Tsuki, who was looking at the ground shyly. They rode in silence as they went.

While not looking up, Tsuki noticed that the inside of the carriage was very ornate, and the seats were quite comfortable. When she entered the carriage, Tsuki noticed the horses were well cared for. The ride wasn't too bumpy, meaning the carriage was well-built.

Tsuki could feel him staring at her like a star in the sky, which made her even more flustered. She had no experience in romance. Sure. Willianna told her everything she knew, but that couldn't hold a candle to the real experience.

The only time Tsuki looked up was when Alistain said, "We are arriving at my castle."

Tsuki saw a large castle on top of a cliff. It and the surrounding forest looked pale in the full moonlight. It had many arches and beautiful glasswork. It was like no castle she had ever seen. She wanted to see the inside and wondered if there was a courtyard just like her castle. She had always loved to play there.

The entrance was enormous but seemed to get even bigger as they went further.

“Wow,” was all Tsuki could say.

Alistain laughed. “Yes, it is quite magnificent. Would you like to see the place I enjoy the most?”

She looked at him with a smile. “Yes, please,” and she followed him into the library. It was dark, only lit by a large fireplace. The walls were lined with books. There was only one chair by the fire.

“Please have a seat,” Alistain said as he motioned for Tsuki to have a seat. “Halt, bring tea,”

Halt bowed, backed away, and left.

Tsuki sat while Alistain stood behind the chair. After a while, he started to play with her hair. He also brushed his cold fingers along the back of her neck. This gave Tsuki goosebumps. She began to blush at his touch. Alistain knew it, too. He went around to the front of the chair.

He placed the back of his hand on her cheek. He leaned in while saying, "Tell me, my dear, what do you see when you look into my eyes? Anger, intrigue, desire?" he went for a kiss.

Tsuki closed her eyes. She had never been kissed like this before, but the anticipation was killing her. She had been told what this meant by Willianna after a local boy asked Tsuki if she had a boyfriend and didn't know what it meant.

Then, as their lips nearly touched, a crash happened outside. Alistain pulled away, stood, and looked out a window. "Now of all times!" He said with an angry look on his face.

Tsuki got up from the chair and walked over to him. "What is it? What happened?"

Alistain turned to leave. "Stay here. Do not go outside," he left, leaving the door open.

Tsuki quickly went after him. She saw him turn to the left, so she followed. She arrived at some large glass doors. She saw Alistain standing, but a large dark figure was before him. It was three times his size. There was a heavy scent of blood. Then she recognized a wolf scent. The large figure was a werewolf; she was almost sure of it.

In the blink of an eye, the fight began. Tsuki then saw the true face of the Count. She stared in awe at the vampire before her. He was matching the large creature blow for blow. He effortlessly dodged the werewolf's attacks, none of them landing.

Then, the werewolf started to speak. "I have no business with you, 'pire," it snarled.

The Count looked puzzled. "Then who are you after?"

Tsuki started to growl. She was beginning to transform. She had mastered her transformation after she had escaped from the compound. It had taken many days to get to where she was comfortable fully transforming.

The werewolf looked at her through the glass door. The Count turned around to look as well. He saw Tsuki, his eyes wide. Tsuki jumped and flew through the glass with her wings to join the Count.

The Count stood in awe. "Wh-what are you?" he asked her.

Before she could answer, the werewolf said, "She is an abomination, and I have been sent to rectify a mistake. I must kill her."

"I will not let that happen," Alistain said as he launched himself at the werewolf. Before he got to the intruder, however, a blur passed him.

It was Tsuki. She was slashing and hacking at the defending werewolf, making blood spray everywhere from his forearms as he defended himself. The werewolf then backstepped and immediately lunged at Tsuki, who dodged.

But, as she and the beast fought, Tsuki's inexperience made her make a tiny but deadly mistake. She was too slow to react to one of his attacks. The werewolf slashed into her, creating a fatal wound. She fell to the ground at Alistain's feet.

Looking at him cloudily, she said, "I-I'm sorry."

This made him furious. The Count released his wrath on the werewolf, killing it in a few seconds by ripping the beast apart, limb from limb.

Covered in blood, Alistain returned to Tsuki, who was dying. She had bled out a lot by now, a pool of her blood forming, mixing with the werewolves. He held her for a few moments and then said, "I'm sorry. I'm so sorry. You weren't supposed to get hurt," tears of blood rolled down his face as he rocked her back and forth, "Tsuki… do you wish to die?"

She shook her head. She couldn't form words, so she mouthed her answer. "No. I want to live."

"Then I shall make you one of my own." He bent down, still holding her tightly, close to her neck. He licked it and then said, "Tsuki, I love you; I have since I first saw you years ago," sinking his fangs into her neck, making a trickle of blood flow down. Now, she was one like him. One of the undead. A vampire.

Chapter Five

Falling

IN THE DAYS following the incident after the ball, Alistain insisted on keeping Tsuki in his castle. Having lost a great deal of blood and in no condition to leave, Tsuki allowed Alistain to fret over her. She made sure to let Willianna know what the situation was.

Willianna, in turn, came to visit Tsuki often. While Tsuki was still bed-bound, she and Willianna had some privacy. This led to many questions from Tsuki's friend about Alistain.

"So what's he like?" Willianna blurted out after checking on her friend for a while.

"Knew that was coming." Tsuki sighed and shook her head.

The older girl raised her hands, "What? You can't expect me to not ask that after everything that's happened."

Tsuki laughed. Her friend always liked gossip and things of that nature.

"Come on," Willianna pleaded with clasped hands, "Is he as suave as he looks? I bet he's a great kisser! Are his teeth sharp since he's a vampire? I bet he is muscular under that shirt."

Placing her hand on her friends, Tsuki quieted Willianna. "Actually, we didn't get much time to, well, do anything before the werewolf attacked."

"Oh, well, that's boring," Willianna said, deflated.

"Ha!" Tsuki laughed, "Sorry, getting attacked by a werewolf and nearly dying before I can kiss a guy is boring to you."

A few weeks had gone by since the ball. Tsuki was still getting used to needing to consume blood. She didn't particularly like having to drink someone's life source, so she and Alistain made a compromise. Since she needed to consume blood to satisfy her vampire attributes but could eat real food, she would be served raw meat. The meat would fill her stomach, and the blood contained in the meat satisfied her vampiric urges.

Now fully recovered, Tsuki had to decide whether she would live in the castle. Willianna wanted her to return to their house. Alistain was adamant about having her stay with him in his castle. But the decision was ultimately up to Tsuki.

As the three sat for dinner, Alistain brought the topic up again. "Have you decided on your living arrangements? Know that no matter what you choose, you will always be welcomed in Castle Valin."

"Thank you, Alistain," Tsuki smiled, dabbing a bit of blood from her mouth with a napkin, "I have. For now, I will stay with Willianna and visit Castle Valin often. Once I feel more comfortable and familiar with us, Alistain, I will decide if I wish to stay in the castle."

Alistain sighed, nodding in defeat. "I understand and will abide by your wishes."

"Yes! Suck that vampire!" Willianna taunted.

"Willianna!" Tsuki exclaimed, getting on to her friend.

Alistain chuckled and leaned on his elbows, which were on the table. "Be careful, human. I am a very patient person. You can't hog Tsuki forever."

Tsuki was soon settled back in the house she shared with Willianna. She had gotten back into her usual routine after a few days when she heard a knock at the door. Opening it, she found Alistain himself waiting under her stoop. He wore a red button-down shirt, black vest and pants, and a wide-brimmed hat with a red feather.

"Alistain? How are you out in the middle of the day? Why are you here?!" Tsuki's eyes widened.

"Heh," chuckled the Count, "Different families of vampires have different resistances to the difficulties of being a creature of the night," he smirked.

"O-oh!" Tsuki blinked, digesting the information.

"Who's at the door?" Willianna called from another room. "Heh, I see your boyfriend is here. You really got it bad, don't you, Alistain. Coming in broad daylight to get your girl," she teased.

At the word "boyfriend," Tsuki blushed.

"Hmm!" Alistain mused at Tsuki getting so flustered. "If I plan on wooing the love of my life, I need to go outside my comfort zone."

"L-I-I...," stuttered Tsuki, an even deeper blush raced across her face. Embarrassed beyond her limits, Tsuki hid her face in her hands.

Alistain smirked, "Ooo, even better!" he exclaimed, clapping once.

Tsuki jumped and let out a high-pitched "Eep!" She fled behind her friend, burying her face into Willianna's shoulder.

"Okay, okay, enough of the cuteness. Why are you here?" the older girl chuckled.

"Oh, that! Well, I was hoping to take dear Tsuki on a picnic. There's a lovely field of flowers near a tree grove with a stream running through it. I thought she might like to see it," Alistain explained softly, extending his hand to Tsuki.

"Well, your Shyness?" Willianna said, looking over her shoulder.

Peeking out from behind her friend, Tsuki looked at Alistain, then his outstretched hand, her face pink as a peach. Coming out from behind Willianna, Tsuki nodded and took the Count's hand with a sweet smile, "Yes, I'd like that."

He had held out his arm for her as they walked. Nearly everything Alistain said to her were comments on her beauty or how happy he was that she had agreed to join him. He even picked her up when they approached a downed tree across the path. Tsuki spent the entire walk with a deep blush on her cheeks.

"Ah, here we are," Alistain said as they approached the treeline.

Looking through the remaining trees, Tsuki spotted the grove Alistain mentioned and, of course, the beautiful field of flowers. Bright colors of purple, red, and white speckled the ground. She could also hear the stream steadily flowing through the tranquil place. "Wow," she exclaimed, "you weren't lying! This place is wonderful!"

"I am glad you are pleased." Alistain hummed as he lightly kissed her hand. "Follow. Let me show you my favorite thing about this place." He guided Tsuki through the grove to the giant tree in the middle. "Shh," he said as he put his finger to his lips. Smiling softly and moving slowly, Alistain made his way to the foot of the massive timber. He looked at something near one of its roots and motioned for Tsuki to join him.

Stepping softly, Tsuki joined her suitor. Looking at the same root, she felt her heart swell. "Awww," Tsuki exclaimed quietly. On the other side of the root, there was a hole in the trunk. Inside was a litter of rabbit kittens. The small animals looked to be a few days old and were asleep.

"I thought the same," Alistain whispered, smiling at the tiny mammals. "We should leave them to rest and find a spot to eat."

Tsuki nodded, and the two made their way out of the grove.

Tsuki had a sudden realization. "Alistain, where is the basket? Or a blanket, for that matter?" she queried, turning to her partner and looking around.

Alistain chuckled, "Don't worry, my dear. I have that taken care of." Extending his arm out to the side, he snapped his fingers together, and a black hole appeared below his hand, crimson particles spinning around the edge. Reaching into the cavity, Alistain pulled out a basket with a blanket on top.

"You can use magic?" Tsuki said, amazed.

"Hmhm," he mused, "some." Setting down the basket, Alistain laid out the blanket.

As he did so, Tsuki looked into the basket to see what was inside. Opening the lid, Tsuki found a stem of grapes, cheese, bread, jam, a wine bottle, and two glasses. Puzzled, she looked at Alistain and said, “Why, there isn’t anything you can have here, Alistain.”

“Not true, my love,” commented the Count. “Vampires can have liquids; it just does not satiate the need we have for blood.”

“I never knew that! My Teacher told me a lot about vampires and the country of Heltavin.” Tsuki told, remembering the many afternoons she spent with Takagi droning on and on about the different countries in Lud.

Alistain nodded, “It’s not widely known among the mortals, but since you are now a vampire, you should know some of these things.”

“Right,” Tsuki concurred.

“All that can come later,” he smiled, “Let us enjoy ourselves and talk about us.” Alistain reached for Tsuki’s hand and ghosted his lips across her knuckles, “Come, sit with me,” his eyes never leaving Tsuki’s.

And that she did. Alistain poured their glasses while Tsuki popped a grape into her mouth. Biting down to let the fruit burst, Tsuki hummed. She couldn’t remember the last time she had felt like this, totally comfortable and safe.

“Here,” Alistain said as he handed her a glass of wine.

Taking it and smelling its contents, Tsuki wrinkled her nose at the smell, looking at Alistain for confirmation. He nodded, so Tsuki shrugged and took a sip. She pondered if she liked it or not and gave it another sip. The sweet liquid agreed with her as she went for another grape.

"How is wine agreeing with you? I know you've never had it before." Alistain commented as he took his own drink.

"Wait, how do you know that?" Tsuki asked excitedly, turning toward her admirer while trying not to spill any drink.

Alistain chuckled. "Well, when I turned you, I saw snippets of your life. And what a difficult one you have had," he commented as he shook his head. Setting down his glass, Alistain cupped Tsuki's cheek, his touch like ice. "I wish to help give you a happy life. From the moment I saw you, I've been spellbound."

"Was that two years ago?" she gasped.

He nodded and took Tsuki's glass away, "I saw you in the market while I was coming through town. You were laughing at something, and I've wanted to steal your heart away ever since." Alistain took her hand and brought it to his lips, "Being your sire is just an added bonus," and then kissed Tsuki's knuckles.

"Oh my." Tsuki breathed as a deep blush grew across her face.

Looking back into her blue-gray eyes with his crimson ones, Alistain captured Tsuki's chin with a firm grasp. Slowly leaning in, he brought his lips to hers. They were cold but incredibly smooth, his mustache tickling her nose.

Returning the kiss, Tsuki let her eyes flutter closed.

Pulling back, Alistain looks at Tsuki with a devious glint in his red orbs. “You are delicious, aren’t you?” Before she had time to think, his lips were on hers again. Alistain picked Tsuki up and placed her in his lap, facing away.

Tsuki let out a yelp as she was lifted, her back flush against her suitor’s front. Her face was covered in a deep blush with doe eyes.

“I’m getting ahead of myself!” Alistain chimed as he wrapped his arms around her middle. “Tell me, my dear,” he said as he put his chin on her head, “What makes you you, hm? What do you aspire to be?”

For the next few hours, Tsuki told him everything, from her favorite color to how she felt about those who acted to hurt her. She had never told anyone everything before, all her trauma, all her fears, about the nightmares she had nightly. But she felt safe with Alistain. She let her guard down for the first time in years, and Alistain knew that by her body language. Tsuki cried about the loss of her parents and how her savior was murdered. She shed tears of rage at the evil doctor who experimented on her for years. She also laughed at times with Kiriuk and Willianna. And through all that, Alistain listened, held her, and wiped away her tears. As the fifth hour started to come to a close, she had eaten all the grapes and most of the bread. And she was utterly spent emotionally.

"Dearest," Alistain mused, "I think I ought to get you home. The sun is setting, and I know I will never hear the end of it if I don't get you back soon."

Looking back at him, Tsuki smiled sheepishly.

Alistain took this opportunity to kiss Tsuki deeply.

"Mumph!" Tsuki exclaimed, and her lips were taken. This allowed Alistain to deepen the kiss even further. After a few moments, Tsuki broke for air.

A chuckle rumbled in Alistain's chest, "You are absolutely divine!"

Chapter Six

Loved and Lost

TSUKI AND ALISTAIN lived together for about two years in Castle Valin once she felt comfortable after several stays. Tsuki was happy and had forgotten about revenge, even though Alistain was very overprotective. He only let her leave the castle under his supervision. So, she had to sneak out frequently. She hadn't gotten caught yet. Tsuki had Willianna to thank for her skills at sneakery.

Tsuki had snuck out to see some of her friends with Willianna and was now coming back. She was scaling the side of the castle to her window like she had done a million times. She got to the window, which she had left open. She climbed through it, shut it, and turned around to climb into bed across the room. But what she saw made her stop.

Alistain was on her bed, lying on his side, facing her. He wore his usual dark suit but had the courtesy to take his shoes off on her bed.

His expression was a cross between anger and intrigue. "Looks like the pup has come back home," Alistain sternly spoke as he sat up, placing his feet on the floor. His long, black hair flowing down his shoulders. "Didn't I tell you to stay on the castle grounds?"

"Wha? How?" Tsuki stammered as Alistain stood.

"I've told you a hundred times, stay on the grounds where I can watch you," Alistain said, raising his voice. He took a step toward Tsuki.

Tsuki quickly recoiled from the Count over the shock of her being found out. "You won't let me do anything! I can't run through the forest or see my friends. I can't even look at the people around in the market! What are you so scared of?"

His face grew angry; a hint of rage built in his eyes but softened into worry. He walked to her. “I’m afraid of losing you,” Alistain said as he brushed a stray hair from her face.

Tsuki looked up at his face. He was smiling sweetly at her. She hugged him, burying her face in his chest. “I would never leave you. The only way we could be separated is by death,” Tsuki’s words were muffled in his chest. But the Count could still hear them as clear as a bell.

They stood there in the pale moonlight in each other’s embrace. Alistain was the one to retract first. “The sun’s almost up. We must rest.”

Tsuki nodded.

As Tsuki got to the bed, Alistain noted, “But, I don’t think I can make it to my chamber. May I stay here with you?” with a devious smile. Alistain had done this many times while Tsuki lived in the castle. He mostly wanted to keep her company and hold her close.

“Sh-sure, if you want. I don’t really care,” Tsuki muttered as she turned away to get into bed. She tried to hide that she was blushing fiercely. No matter how often he asked, she still would get flustered at the idea of sharing a bed with him. She was also constantly teased by Willianna about it.

She climbed into her king-sized bed, the biggest one she’d ever slept in. It had silk sheets and pillows as fluffy as marshmallows. She loved it but didn’t like how it was huge compared to just her.

Once she had gotten settled, she felt cold hands glide over her. Her skin tingled from his touch, and she felt his breath on the back of her neck, giving her goosebumps. Then his hand started to wander. Gliding along her stomach, her arms, and her legs. He pressed his body against her back. Tsuki jumped when she felt the bare skin of his chest.

Alistain felt her jump; smiling, he gently pulled her closer. "Shhh, it's okay. I won't hurt you," he then licked from the base of her neck to the lobe of her ear. "You're so fragile; it feels like if I hold you too tightly, I might break you in half," Alistain whispered into her ear, "You are mine and mine alone." He kissed her neck and slid his hand along Tsuki's arm. This made her shiver. But at the last second, Tsuki stopped him. He sighed. "Not tonight, huh. Cuddling it is then."

They lay there for the rest of the night in each other's embrace. Tsuki's warmth and Alistain's cold.

The next day, Tsuki woke to the bright light of midday. Her eyes squinted from the light. She glanced over her shoulder to look for the Count, but he was nowhere to be seen.

Tsuki stood and stretched her limbs. She yawned loudly as she stretched. Her stomach growled with a low rumble. "Right, I haven't had lunch yet," She grabbed her robe on the post at the end of the bed and made her way to the main dining hall, where Halt had lunch prepared for her. Like always, she was dining alone. Her meal consisted of a roasted deer, a small salad, and part of a fresh loaf of bread. Her wine glass was filled with the blood of the deer she was eating.

As she happily ate her meal, Alistain quietly snuck up behind her. Brushing her hair away from her neck, he leaned down close and said, “Hungry today, are we?” kissing her neck as she swallowed a bite of deer, his kiss lingering.

She quickly wiped her mouth and turned to look up at the Count. When she did, her lips met his. As he pulled away, he licked his lip. “Mmm, wonderful. The taste of your meal lingers on your lips,” he mused as he wiped a bit of blood that she had missed from the corner of her mouth.

As he licked his finger, she said, “And here I thought you wanted to taste me,” with a mischievous grin on the edge of her lips.

He laughed to himself for a few seconds. He pulled a chair close to where she was sitting. She returned to eating. He sat and watched her with happy eyes. After a few minutes of silence, Alistain finally said, “What do you think about going out tonight?” with a side glance.

Tsuki had barely finished her meal and looked up abruptly at the Count. “Really? Are we going to the dance in the square?” she said excitedly, nearly jumping out of her chair. It had been months since Alistain had taken her to a dance.

The Count chuckled as he nodded his head.

Tsuki jumped up from her chair to leave. “Then I need to pick a dress!”

He stood as she left. “I bought you a new one. It’s in your room on the bed. I hope you’ll like it,” he called after her as she left, nearly running.

When Tsuki got to her room, just like Alistain had said, a brand-new dress was lying on her bed.

As she got closer to look at the dress, she gasped. The dress was a replica of the one he got her years ago when they first met: a dark blue dress trimmed with silver. The shoulders were silver-trimmed blue. As she picked it up, she didn’t notice that he was standing in the doorway.

“As you guessed. It’s the same as the first. The one that started it all,” he said as he walked over to her. “It took a long time to track down the man who made the first. But I managed to get it. I thought you would want another since the original was torn to shreds by that furry monster,” He put his arm around her waist.

“I love it!” she said in joy. “It’s perfect. Are you going to wear the same as that night?” Tsuki turned to look at him.

Alistain laughed to himself. “I wouldn’t have it any other way,” he cooed, kissing her deeply.

She looked into his eyes and laid her head on his chest. He wrapped his arms around her waist and set his chin on her head. They stood there for a few minutes. They parted once they saw the sun start to go down.

“Get ready and meet me in the library when you are done,” Alistain said, leaving the room.

An hour later, Tsuki walked slowly down the spiral stairs. The Count was there waiting for her.

"You look absolutely stunning," he uttered, kissing her hand gently. "Are you ready to go?"

Tsuki nodded and followed him to the door where Halt had the carriage waiting.

As they rode, Alistain never looked away from Tsuki. She could feel his eyes on her, but she was used to it. He tended to lovingly stare at her like she was the only thing in the room. It made Tsuki feel special.

The carriage slowed as they neared the square. When Tsuki stepped out of the carriage, the people nearby turned and stared at her and the Count. They were whispering.

"Don't worry about them. Let them say what they want," Alistain voiced as he placed an arm around her waist. He led her to the center area, where the dancing was. "Milady, may I have this dance?" He held his hand out.

Tsuki placed her hand in his as they walked to the dance floor. Trying to ignore the strange glances from the crowd, Tsuki focused on the music and Alstain. Soon, all her worries faded away.

They danced till near the end of the night when someone yelled, "There he is!"

The crowd parted to show two men. One burly-looking man who was gigantic in both stature and muscle. He carried a sword in his hand. The other man held a book to his chest and was pointing at the two of them.

"Hurry!" Alistain yelled as he nearly dragged Tsuki to the carriage. "As fast as you can, old friend," he breathed to Halt as they got in. Halt sped down the road up to the castle. The Count kept looking behind them to see if they were being followed, but no one was in sight.

"What's going on? Tell me, who were those men," Tsuki pleaded.

The Count turned to look at her with a grave face. "They're vampire hunters," he said bluntly. "Once we get to the castle, go into the library; you'll be safe there. If they come in, hide. Don't worry about me. Halt, and I will try to fight them off. But if we fail, leave here and go to a different country. Because they will hunt you down," Alistain stated sternly.

Halt drove the carriage as fast as possible to escape the assailants running to get their horses. This reminded Tsuki of the time Takagi had gotten her and her parents away from a group of bandits. He had risked his life that day, and Halt was doing the same.

"B-but I don't want to leave you," Tsuki cried.

Alistain kissed her forehead. "You have to be brave. If you were hurt, I don't know what I'd do."

When they arrived at the castle, Alistain yelled, "Go! Run!" and pushed Tsuki out of the carriage. She looked back, and his face was sad.

Tsuki did as she was told and retreated to the dark library, where there were many places to hide. She could hear talking outside the window. It was three men; one of the voices was the Count's.

Tsuki walked over to find Alistain facing two other men with weapons. The man closest to the Count had a long leather trenchcoat with many weapons in his belt. He had blonde hair that went to his shoulders but a light brown beard that reminded her of the werewolf man she had lived with all those years ago. It was hard to see much of his face from the angle Tsuki was looking at.

They had swords, guns, torches, stakes, and lances. All weapons for fighting a vampire. She watched in awe as the three men stood, waiting for the other to move. She looked on the ground and saw a body lying on the ground. It was Halt! He was lying in a large pool of blood.

She tried to focus on his body, but her attention was drawn by the others beginning to fight. They were dashing around, slashing each other, and barely missing each time. After the burst of violence, they paused.

"Why have you followed me here? Who are you?" Alistain yelled at the stranger.

The other man just laughed. "I guess I can give you the courtesy. I am Abraham Whitiker, the man who will kill you," Without warning, Whitiker launched himself at Alistain, slashing wildly.

"Kill me? Never, I have too much to lose to let you win," The Count shouted mockingly.

They seemed evenly matched at first, but Tsuki could see that the Count was losing. It wasn't noticeable to regular people, but for people trained to fight, the gradual slowing of the Count was all too clear. Then, out of nowhere, Whitiker landed a hit across Alistain's chest, spraying blood on the ground.

"Damn you. You're using a blessed sword," Alistain cursed. Usually, his wounds would begin to heal almost immediately. But because the sword was blessed, he couldn't heal it. "This is getting interesting." He said with a huge smile as he launched himself at Whitiker.

As they clashed, Alistain faltered again. Whitiker slashed him three times across his chest before he could escape. Alistain stepped back and found himself blocked by a wall of the castle. He was trapped.

Alistain looked at the wall. "Well, it looks like I won't be able to keep my promise to her. Damn it."

Whitiker looked at him. "Her? There is no way that a heartless wretch like you could have someone he cares for," he pulled out a stake from his coat walking toward the Count.

Alistain laughed. "That's what I thought at first, but then I learned more and more about her. And before I knew it, I had fallen in love," His face softened as he talked.

"Well, I am sorry for her because it changes nothing. I still have to fulfill my mission to kill you," Whitiker raised the stake to strike Alistain's heart. He threw it, piercing the Count, who cried out in pain.

Alistain hunched over in defeat. He then started to cry tears of blood. They were streaking down his face. Then, through tears, he said, "All I wish is to see her face one last time. My dear Tsuki."

As Tsuki watched the battle close, she started to cry. She couldn't hear what they were saying but didn't care. It took almost all her strength not to rush out there to save the Count. But his words rang in her ears, "If you were hurt, I don't know what I'd do."

She couldn't take any more of this; she couldn't watch the life drain out of his body. Tsuki turned away, ran up to her room on the other side of the castle, and picked out a few things she would need. She was going to run, just like her love told her to. She packed clothes for the journey and her father's sword.

Once she gathered everything, she scaled down the side of the castle; it would be too risky to go out any of the exits near the battle. And as she touched the ground, she looked back up to her window. "Goodbye, my love. I swear I will live like you wished me to," she said, running into the dense woods.

Unbeknownst to Tsuki after the battle, Whitiker walked up to Alistain and knelt to where they were at eye level, “Do you care for her enough to give up everything?”

Alistain raised his head to meet eye-to-eye with him, “Yes, I would. She is my life. The only one that matters.”

Whitiker smiled and looked like he was about to laugh. “Well then. If I spare you, for as long as my family lives, you shall be our slave. Do we have an accord?”

Alistain's eyes widened. “If I give you my freedom, I might be able to see her again?”

Whitiker nodded.

“Then I give it to you without hesitation. We shall seal it in our blood,” Alistain said breathlessly as he placed a hand on his chest that was covered in blood, as Whitiker took out a knife and sliced his hand. Then they clasped hands, sealing the agreement with a blood pact.

Whitiker pulled the stake out of the Count's chest.

And after he winced, Alistain looked up to see a full moon. “Tsuki, my love. I know that we shall meet again someday.”

Chapter Seven

Homeward Bound

TSUKI KEPT RUNNING until she came to a clearing. She stopped to rest and collapsed to the ground, sobbing. The one good thing in her life was gone again. First, her parents and Takagi, then Alpha and Kiriuk, and now Alistain and Willianna.

Through her sobs, she heard rustling in the trees across the clearing from her. There was a man clad in silver and dark blue. He looked familiar. Tsuki stood and readied for battle.

"Tsuki?" asked the man as he came slowly forward.

Immediately, she recognized him as Kiriuk. She used the last of her strength to run to him.

"Kiriuk? Is that really you, brother?" she asked. He had grown so much since she last saw him. He looked like a proper man now instead of the goofy kid she knew from before.

Kiriuk, now taller than Tsuki, wore a gray tunic with blue trim and a long gray coat with his tail poking out the back. He also wore a spiked necklace and carried a spear on his back. He had on boots that looked like they were well-worn.

As she hugged Kiriuk, she saw movement behind him and recognized her old childhood Teacher, Takagi.

He was dressed in all blue. A dark blue button-up shirt and a light blue waistcoat with tails lined in dark blue. His pants were striped with alternating light and dark blue. Even his shoes were blue. His long hair was blue, just as his eyes were. And those were framed by round glasses fitted on his face. Everything about him was as she had remembered.

"Takagi!" She exclaimed and ran over to the blue-haired man.

"My lady! I can't believe it's you," Takagi exclaimed as he knelt before Tsuki could hug him. "I have been searching all the neighboring countries for you. I knew you weren't killed that day. You were always a resourceful child."

As Takagi stood, Tsuki noticed a tear in his eye. He looked weary but joyful at the same time. Tsuki then pushed the formalities aside and hugged the wizard.

"How did you come across Kiriuk?" Tsuki asked, looking back at Kiriuk.

"I ran to the castle after father died. And I ran into Takagi there and told him about what had happened and about you. He immediately put the two stories together, and we've been trying to find you ever since," Kiriuk cheered as his tail wagged.

Tsuki wiped her face of tears with her sleeve and softly smiled at the two. They were brimming with happiness and excitement while she was anything but.

“What’s wrong sis? Did I say something wrong?” Kiriuk jumped when he saw Tsuki’s teary eyes.

Tsuki explained what had happened to her since she had last seen Kiriuk. It took her some time to recover after recounting what had happened to her love, and they camped in that clearing for the night. Kiriuk and Takagi took shifts to keep Tsuki safe so that she could rest.

And thus, the three headed off to confront Tsuki's uncle. She was stronger now, and with the help of her friends, she believed she could talk him down. Kiriuk and Takagi wanted a harsher punishment for her uncle, but ultimately, it was her decision.

Tsuki changed out of her dress and was now clad in a gray shirt trimmed with green and black pants and a blue coat with red fur around the edges. It was an outfit that Willianna had given her for one of her birthdays. Her father's sword rested on her hip.

From the clearing, the three made their way from the mountain that held the castle town where Tsuki had lived for the past 4 years. It was lonely for Tsuki, especially as she realized she was leaving her best friend, Willianna, behind. Being unable to tell her where she was going and that she was safe hurt.

As they walked, Kiriuk kept the conversation going as he asked many questions and told stories from his time searching for her with Takagi. Any time Takagi had an input, he followed it with an apology for taking so long to find her. After the third time, Tsuki stopped him mid-sentence.

Tsuki turned to him with a hand on his shoulder. “Takagi, you could not know where I had fled after the attack. You had no idea I had been kidnapped for so long. And you did not know I was in that secluded castle town. But you definitely don’t deserve any blame for all that has happened to me. Okay?” her voice was gentle, as sadness filled her eyes. She had no idea of his pain from the blame he obviously placed upon himself, but she knew he didn’t deserve any of it.

Takagi stood in shock for a few seconds, not knowing how to react. Then, his stoic features crumpled, and tears filled his eyes. “I… You… Thank you, little one,” Takagi stuttered as tears fell. He then took a knee and bowed his head. “I pledge my loyalty to you, Princess Tsuki Mage of Urufu. You will have my aid until I depart for the stars like those before me.”

It was Tsuki’s turn to be in shock. She turned to Kiriuk to alleviate the tension, but he, too, was kneeling.

“My loyalty is yours; we will have each other till the day I am slain,” Kiriuk said, his tail wagging.

Tsuki looked at her friends, no, her family. A smile graced her face as tears streamed down her cheeks. “Rise, my dear companions. From this day on, Takagi, you will be my right hand and Kiriuk, you will be my left. Your existence is an extension of myself. Hold yourselves with the appropriate authority.”

They passed through a small city on their journey to the Urufian capital. The trio was very thankful to have an actual bed and a warm meal in their stomachs while at an inn. They had entered the city after dusk and dragged themselves to the inn's tavern. All three sighed as they sat, their feet crying when their weight was removed. They had taken many backroads to this city and had crossed the border between Heltavin and Urufu. It was a lot of rugged paths and uneven footing.

“Ahh,” sighed Kiriuk, “finally back home. And a warm place to sleep, too. I bet I will sleep like a rock!"

A barmaid gave them a hot bowl of stew and some ale for a few coins. Takagi gave her a 'thank you.' The three scarfed down their food and drink, even paying for seconds. After they were finished, each sat back in their chair, content with a full belly.

As Tsuki started to say something to her friends, a group of loud men burst through the tavern's entrance.

"Five meals and keep the ale coming!" said one of the large, rough-looking men as they sat at a table in the middle of the floor.

Takagi sighed, shook his head, "We should probably call it a night," and stood.

Tsuki and Kiriuk also stood, and the three started to the inn portion of the structure.

As the trio passed by the rowdy table of men, Tsuki heard a whistle in her direction. She ignored it and kept walking.

"Hey, puppy girl! I'm talking to you!" the large man who called for the food growled. He stood and chased after Tsuki and her group as they walked away, grabbing her arm to spin her around.

"Hey!" Tsuki shouted as she was yanked backward. Her friends stopped to see what was happening, Kiriuk bearing his fangs and Takagi reaching for his magic book.

The tall man chuckled as he towered over the short Tsuki. "Why don't you stick around with me and my buddies? We can show you a good time. Better than those sissy boys you have with you." He laughed, not letting go of Tsuki's arm, holding it tightly.

Tsuki laughed, ripping her arm out of his strong grasp. "You should spend more time on your manners and a bath rather than partying. If you touch me again, you will lose an arm. Learn common decency and brush your teeth, and then we'll talk." She then turned and joined her friends.

"No one talks to me like that! Get back here!" the man yelled, reaching for Tsuki's shoulder.

In a flash, Tsuki launched herself backward, jumping over the man, grabbing his head, and throwing him against the wall of the tavern, sufficiently knocking out the man. She then looked over to his friends, none standing to fight her as they sat in stunned silence.

Tsuki chuckled, "That's what I thought."

Takagi and Kiriuk stood in awe of their compatriot. Kiriuk let out a bark of a laugh and patted Tsuki on her shoulder.

As the three walked up to their rooms, Takagi spoke, stunned at what he had witnessed, “My lady, I had no idea you could fight like that. It was impressive, to say the least.”

“A lot has changed, Teacher,” Tsuki said as her gaze looked distant, “but I’m glad to be going to where I belong, home.” A soft smile graced her lips as she turned away to climb the stairs.

The next day, as the trio left the inn to find supplies and return to the road, they ran into the rowdy group of men from the previous night. It looked like they were roughing up a local shopkeeper.

“We should help the poor guy out,” Tsuki instructed as she shook her head.

The three walked up to the scene of the men surrounding the shopkeep that they had lifted in the air.

"Now, I won't repeat myself again. Give us all yer gold, and we won't have to hurt ya," growled the group leader.

Tsuki cleared her throat, making the band of men look at her. "I would say it's nice to see you again, but I don't like lying. How about you let the nice man down, leave this town, and get lost. That way, I don't have to cut your hands off."

"You three can't take all seven of us!" shouted one of the men. The rest agreed.

Tsuki looked to her friends and then back at the hostile group, slowly approaching them and pulling their weapons out. "Remember, try to leave them with their lives."

"Are you sure, my lady? Someone of your status shouldn't worry yourself with trivial matters like this," Takagi commented as he brought out his book.

Tsuki turned to Takagi and smiled, "If I let this stand, then I might as well condone it. Turning a blind eye to suffering only creates room for more suffering. If we nip it in the bud here, they are less likely to do it later." As she finished her remark, one man launched at her. Tsuki stepped to the side and stuck her foot out, making the man tumble and land on his face. "Besides, I think this fight is happening no matter what we do."

"See, wizard, I told you she was wicked smart! And she's super strong, too!" Kiriuk boasted as he brought out his spear.

“Nah, they are just really predictable,” Tsuki chuckled as the man who had charged at her stood and took a swing at her with his knife, which she blocked.

“Ahhhh! Get ‘em!” yelled the group's leader.

Opening his book, Takagi recited an earth-throwing spell, the page glowing green, sending medium-sized rocks at the two men approaching him. One rock connected with one of their heads, knocking the man out cold. Takagi put up a shield spell just in time for a blow of the other man’s sword to bounce off of the magic barrier. Quickly dropping his shield, Takagi kicked the man squarely in the chest, sending him backward and onto the ground.

Kiriuk had three men rush him, spreading out as they went. “You guys think you’re the top dog? Well, let a real wolf show you how it’s done,” he chuckled as he spun his spear in one hand. One man charged, and Kiriuk swiftly hit him on the head with the end of his spear, knocking the man out. As he finished with the first, a second came from the side with his sword out. Kiriuk used the momentum from the first strike to knock the man's sword down and out of his hand. Then Kiriuk planted the butt of the spear in the ground and jumped, bringing a foot to kick the man back and to the ground. As he pushed off the second attacker, Kiriuk flipped and brought the end of the spear to the third assailant’s shoulder, thus incapacitating that arm, which was holding a club. When the one he had kicked tried to get up, Kiriuk pointed his spearhead at the man's throat, making him freeze.

The last of the goons, the leader, took a few swings at Tsuki. She ducked under the attacks, slid past the man's legs, and got behind him. She kicked him in the back, which sent him tumbling into his boss. The thugs went toppling over each other and finally found the ground. "And that is how you disarm a bunch of pompous thugs."

The shopkeeper ran up to Tsuki from hiding behind his wagon, "My word! That was incredible! Thank you so very much! How can I repay you and your friends?"

"No reward is needed," Tsuki said as she waved a dismissive hand, "just, please get the constabulary and get these idiots in a jail cell. Maybe then they will learn their lesson."

A look of surprise came across the shopkeeper's face, "O-okay, of course."

Takagi put his hand on Tsuki's shoulder as the three walked away. "You have grown into an amazing, strong, and beautiful young woman. I can't wait to see what you will do during your reign." He had a look of fondness in his eyes. "Now, onto the capital," he said as he let his hand slide down Tsuki's arm and grazed her hand.

Chapter Eight

Confrontation?

ENTERING THE CASTLE town, there were many run-down huts and houses, and the people in them looked thin, tired, and dirty.

"What happened?" asked Tsuki, her heart in her throat with sadness.

Takagi shook his head, "After your uncle took the throne, several motions passed that took money from the infrastructure budget and fed it into other things, like magic items and the military."

While they walked closer to the castle, a little girl ran after a ball that bounced in front of the trio. "Hey, oh! Sorry, I was just chasing my ball."

Tsuki looked at the girl; she was very malnourished and had tattered clothes that looked to be made with a sack that once held flour. Her ball was also torn up, barely held together by adhesive paste and leather. "It's okay," Tsuki said as she crouched down to her level. "Can I ask you a question?"

"Yeah!" exclaimed the girl.

"When did you eat last?" Tsuki queried.

The little girl thought for a moment, "Yesterday morning." She looked sad.

"Okay," Tsuki said as she thought, "How many people are in your family?"

The little girl tilted her head and looked at Tsuki. "Four, it's my mom and me and my two brothers," commented the girl, "Why?"

Tsuki turned to Takagi, who was already looking through his purse bag, understanding what Tsuki was doing. Takagi handed Tsuki a few silver coins and nodded.

Holding the coins out to the girl, Tsuki smiled, "Here you go, sweety."

The little girl gasped, "But that's too much money, lady! You shouldn't give me all that! Mom will probably make me give it back anyway."

“I promise she won’t get mad,” Tsuki chuckled, “Take the money, hold it close to your chest, and go find your mom, okay?”

The little girl nodded slowly and hesitantly took the silver, running off immediately into a sea of dilapidated houses. “Mommy! Mommy!”

As they approached the castle, Tsuki's heart dropped. The castle was in shambles and less magnificent than she remembered.

The guards at the castle let Takagi in but barred Tsuki and Kiriuk from entering. They blocked the way and separated Takagi and his companions.

“Sorry, folks. Only known castle staff is allowed in without an invitation,” commented the guard on the right.

"You fools! Don't you know your princess when you see her?" Takagi exclaimed in outrage. How dare they bar Tsuki entrance. They will hear it from their commander later, he thought.

"What? You mean the lost princess?" one of the guards said.

“There’s no way the lost princess is that girl. It's probably just some fake. I mean, hells, she’s a werewolf,” the other guard laughed as he eyed Tsuki.

“How dare you insinuate that I’m lying. I, of all people, would know who the princess is,” Takagi commented, a little taken aback.

The first guard raised an eyebrow, “Weren’t you run out of town and told to never return?”

Takagi’s eyes turned a dangerous blue, and in them was a rage that Tsuki hadn’t seen since she was little. “I am the royal advisor and court magician.”

“Were!” added the second guard.

Takagi's glare made the guards shrink in fear, “I do not see that man as my king, and you would do well to think the same. I have with me the lost princess, and you will give us entry.”

"Well, if sir Takagi says it's true, it must be, right?" the first guard said as he shakily held his spear...

"I guess so," said the second guard hesitantly.

They let the trio in as Tsuki's heart sped up. She was actually going to do it. She was going to confront her uncle.

Once they entered the castle's great hall, Takagi approached a group of men wearing regal robes. The robes were all white and floor-length. They were actually thrown over regular clothes. She recognized them as the council of nine, the main legislative body of Urufu.

Tsuki stared as Takagi walked up and whispered to the man with the largest hat. The hat was long and cylindrical, with a point at the top. He turned to look at Tsuki. He smiled and said, "Brothers and sisters, we are blessed to have our princess return to us!"

The small group and literally everyone in the hall turned to look at Tsuki. She had never been timid about things in public, but having everyone stare at her in unison made her feel very small.

"Umm..." Tsuki said as she stood still, trying to make herself smaller.

That's when she heard people talking.

"Is that really her?"

"Is that the lost princess?"

"That can't be her."

"She looks nothing like the pictures."

“I bet she’s a fake who just wants money.”

That was the last straw. Tsuki had had enough of those belittling her. She cleared her throat and put her right hand over her heart in a fist, as was the customary salute in Urufu. "My name is Tsuki Mage! And I am the princess of Urufu!" She yelled. “Besides, how would I have this if I wasn’t the princess?” Tsuki announced as she held up her father's sword.

All at once, there was a loud murmur in the crowd. Then, in unison, the crowd knelt down before her. Even Takagi and Kiriuk knelt. She finally felt like she was where she belonged, like she was home.

Then, off to the side, there was the sound of metal clanging together, a group of soldiers arriving moments after the sound started, growing louder. They rushed into the hall and stood at the ready.

Behind the soldiers came an older gentleman dressed in regal attire. He was blonde-headed with gray streaks, shaved cheeks, and tufts of hair. His jaw was bordered by gray mutton chops. He had on a cape that had fur on the shoulders and trimmed with the same fur. It was bright blue, immediately marking him as royalty. He had the Urufian crown on his head. It was a dome with two leaves of fabric on the left and right with a silver spike on top. It was lined with jewels, and in the center of it all was a moonstone, the Urufian jewel. That was Tsuki's uncle, Lentus.

"What's the meaning of all this shouting?" Lentus demanded.

That's when everyone got up off their knees and continued murmuring.

"I said, what is going on here?!" Lentus said louder.

"Oh, my liege! You will be delighted to hear that-eh?" the council leader voiced with joy as Tsuki's uncle cut him off.

"I wasn't talking to you. And you!" Lentus spat as he shoved his hand in the face of a councilman, not even the one talking. He then strode over to Takagi and poked him in his chest. "I thought the traitor wasn't supposed to come back?"

"He's with me," Tsuki spoke sternly and with force. Seeing the regal man, her uncle, made her blood boil.

"And who, the hell, are you?" her uncle said pointedly. He strode over to Tsuki with his long legs.

As he stood nose to nose with her, all she could think about was what he would do once he figured out who she was. She was ready for a fight but doubted it would come to that.

"Hello, uncle," Tsuki said softly. "You haven't changed a bit."

All the blood drained from her uncle's face. He took a step backward. It took him a few moments to think of what to do, and he looked around and saw how many people were there.

"Tsuki! Niece!" he voiced in mock excitement. Her uncle then wrapped his arms around Tsuki in a one-sided hug and said through clenched teeth, "I thought you were dead."

"Well, I'm not, uncle. I'm so glad to see your rescue party finally found me." Tsuki said flatly, pointing to Takagi as she shook her uncle off.

"Well, of course! Only the best to find our princess, eh?" Lentus spoke meekly as he let go of Tsuki. He walked around her, looking at everyone like he was being truthful. Like he hadn't just insulted Takagi and called him a traitor.

"So, how did you survive?" asked one of the councilmen.

"Yes, how did you?" asked her uncle in what seemed to be anger.

“It must have been a miracle from the gods,” Tsuki announced to the crowd. “I know not how I survived, but I did. And I have had multiple trials since.”

“Well, it's great to have you back!” one of the councilmen said, breaking the tension. The crowd, who had congregated closer to the king and Tsuki, quietly agreed.

Tsuki looked around and made sure that the people were paying attention. She was going to call out her uncle right there. "I know what you've done, uncle." Tsuki threatened.

One of the councilmen approached the two, who were in heated eye contact. "Oh! So, you know how he found the loophole in the treaty with Heltavin and saved us thousands of gold?"

"He did what now?" Tsuki asked in disbelief.

"Yeah, I found an error your mother made in that piece of scratch. Now we're much better off without them." Lentus laughed haughtily, crossing his arms.

No wonder Heltavians scoffed at her when she told them she was Urufian. They were swindled out of a deal centuries in the making. All for a few measly bits of gold. This may be why everything appeared so run down. It was all her uncle's doing, trying to accumulate more gold.

This realization filled Tsuki with rage. How could her people be so blind to this man grabbing for power and gold? They were being used and tossed to the side when they weren't useful anymore. His body count must be extensive.

"He even expanded our armies! Your cousin, Clarent, is leading them on a campaign to conquer the surrounding nations." mentioned another councilman.

All the blood drained from her face. He had turned Tsuki's peaceful home into a war state. This was ridiculous. All because he wanted more power. It must be evident to the councilmen what was going on with his treatment of them. While yes, they are a major body in governing Urufu, the monarchy can outweigh their decision. "But I thought we were known to be a diplomatic nation?" asked Tsuki, not directing her comment at anyone.

"Yes, we were, but our people are much happier this way. And I'm sure those former nations we have taken over are much better off. Right, my liege?" asked the head councilman with a frightened look.

Lentus was using his power to do whatever he wanted, and in the process, ruined Tsuki's country by terrorizing the other countries. He smiled proudly at the mention of his son and the changes he had made, completely ignoring Tsuki and her companions. "Quite right, quite right. Much better off," he said, laughing.

Tsuki had half a mind to stab her uncle right there with her father's sword but decided that without any evidence and with his firm hold on people, it would be disastrous for her. So, she formed a quick plan of action and carried it out. She would fill Takagi and Kiriuk in later and flesh it out in more detail.

"Well, I can see you've been busy, uncle. I wish I had more time to listen to what you've done, but my companions and I are exhausted from our long journey and would like to rest," Tsuki said. It wasn't entirely false, but she needed to talk with her friends to finish her plan.

"Oh, of course! You must be tired and don't want everything thrown at you at once, eh?" Lentus said, clapping his hands at several men dressed similarly to Takagi. They were obviously servants. "Take the…princess and her friends to rooms and make them comfortable. That is all!" he commanded the servants.

The servants bowed and stepped toward Tsuki. One said, “Right this way, your highness.”

Tsuki and her friends quickly followed after the one who had spoken as he swiftly walked away.

As soon as they were out of earshot of the king and those in the great hall, Takagi spoke up for the first time since this whole thing began. “Reginald!” Takagi declared as he fell in step with the one leading the group. “Has the king gone mad? And what happened to all the rest of us?”

Reginald stopped and looked Takagi dead in the eye. “We do not speak ill of the king. Perpetrators do not return. Best keep quiet and keep your head down. The same goes for you, princess. I'd hate for you to get hurt.”

His words were chilling. That's why Tsuki didn't recognize any of the staff and barely any of the councilmen. Her uncle had killed them all off to keep power. After realizing this, Tsuki knew she had to act fast to right her uncle's wrongs. Otherwise, she would be dead, just like her parents.

Once they got to her chambers, Tsuki told Takagi and Kiriuk to return to her once they had found their rooms. They quietly nodded, understanding that she had a plan for them but couldn't speak about it with company loyal to the king.

Tsuki entered her room for the first time in over thirteen years. It was immaculately kept, and no speck of dust was anywhere, probably Takagi’s orders. It was just as she had left it that morning so long ago. Her afternoon clothes for that day were still hanging up by her closet. This made memories of a distant life run through Tsuki's mind. She began to tear up. She then took a ragged breath, shut her eyes tightly, and wiped away her tears. She didn't have time to reminisce. If she was going to defeat her uncle, she needed to stay focused.

She was about to find a pen and paper in her room when there was a knock at the door. She turned and readied herself for whoever came through. “Come in,” she called as she reached behind her for her sword.

Takagi stepped into the room, and Tsuki relaxed. “I'm glad you're ready for anything, my lady,” he chuckled after seeing her hand release the hilt.

Kiriuk soon followed Takagi in entering the room. “Sorry,” Kiriuk apologized, “I kind of got lost. This place is massive.”

“Don't apologize, brother. You've never been here, so how should you know your way around?” Tsuki laughed as she clasped a hand onto Kiriuk’s shoulder, Happy to see him safe once again.

Chapter Nine

Clever Girl

THE SUN HAD gone down, and it was late into the night. Everything was wrapping up. Everyone in the castle was getting ready for the night shifts or settling into bed. All except for Tsuki and her team. They were just getting started.

Tsuki had explained her rudimentary plan to her two friends. And thankfully, with their tactical knowledge, they formulated the plan to dethrone King Lentus. It wouldn't be easy, and timing was vital. Tsuki just hoped it wouldn't end in a fight.

She slowly made her way to the throne room. She didn't hide where she was going and even loudly asked one of the maids which way it was. This was all going according to her plan.

Once she arrived, she saw her uncle and Kiriuk discussing hunting techniques. Her uncle was a great sportsman and had won many trophies. She had once looked up to her uncle. Now, all she felt was hatred and disdain.

"Ah, there she is," Kiriuk exclaimed as he motioned to Tsuki as she entered.

"About time," muttered Lentus. Once Tsuki got near enough, he called her. "Ah, good. Now, won't you leave us, Sir Kiriuk?"

Kiriuk bowed and quickly turned to leave.

Once he was gone from the room, Lentus cleared his throat. "So, what was so important that you kept me up? I'm not getting any younger. I need my rest."

"I understand, uncle, but we needed to discuss this. I know who killed my parents," Tsuki said flatly, staring Lentus in the eye.

Again, his face went pale, and he took a moment to find his words. "You do? Who?"

"Well," Tsuki continued, "I know who ordered the killing."

There was a long beat of silence. Lentus stood with bated breath for Tsuki to tell him who she thought it was. She wanted to give her friends time to work.

"Uncle, it was you. Wasn't it?" Tsuki finally said softly.

"W-what? Those were just silly rumors." Lentus said nervously.

"Really? Then why are you charging a spell behind your back?" Tsuki asked sharply.

Tsuki quickly jumped backward to avoid getting hit by a fireball that came out of Lentus' hand as he swung it forward.

"Why are you attacking me, uncle? If you have nothing to hide, then there is nothing to be afraid of," Tsuki mocked as she pulled her sword out from behind her. She was used to fighting with her claws but had always trained with the sword.

"That sword! So you are the real thing," Lentus said as he threw a lightning bolt at Tsuki, barely missing her.

"So, you did kill them. And then you tried to have me killed again by hiring a werewolf mercenary!" Tsuki yelled as she dodged another blow. "But this was after you knew that I was the test subject of that monster doctor!"

"So, what if I killed them and tried to kill you? You're nothing but a pain in my side. A mistake that needs to be corrected!" Lentus spewed as he threw another bolt of lightning in Tsuki's direction.

"That's all I needed to hear," Tsuki said smugly. She then expertly threw her sword at her uncle. The blade flew through the air and caught on Lentus' robe, pulling him backward. He was now pinned against the throne and couldn't get free. As soon as he knew he was pinned, Lentus began to panic and threw spell after spell around the room.

"You won't get away with this, you abomination! I will conquer this continent and have all the power!" Tsuki's uncle screamed. "I will kill you, and no one will know!" At that moment, he tore free from the sword that held him against the stone.

"Oh really?" Tsuki chuckled. She snapped her fingers and Lentus was suddenly bound to the throne by a strong magic.

"What? Who?" Lentus asked, panicking as he looked around for the wizard who had bound him.

Takagi stepped out from behind the throne, his magic book glowing and floating above his hand. "Stay still, won't you?" Takagi commented mockingly.

Lentus, still able to move his arms, flew spell after spell at Tsuki, with her deftly dodging. He then blasted a spell near Takagi, making the wizard dodge, thus losing his concentration and dropping the spell holding Lentus. Falling from the holding spell, Lentus stumbled and ran 50 yards from Tsuki. "You can't do this! The power is mine! I won't let you take this away from me! You won't take away what's rightfully mine!"

Using her superior speed, Tsuki was behind her uncle in a flash. "You really are pathetic, a disgrace of our name," she then reared back and punched Lentus square in the back, sending him flying all the way back to the throne, landing in the seat.

Takagi took this opportunity to put his holding spell back on the shambles of a man.

Tsuki approached the throne and grabbed her sword from the stone slab at the back. Since it was deeply embedded, Tsuki used most of her strength to pull it out. Once it was free, she aimed the tip at the throat of her uncle.

“I should kill you right now. But… I…” Tsuki said as she trailed off into her own thoughts. She let the tip of her blade falter downwards.

“You have every right to decree his execution, princess. He has controlled us all and only thought of himself,” announced the head councilman as he walked into the room, followed by the rest of the council and Kiriuk. Tsuki looked at them and smiled once she saw her friend.

“You clever girl. You planned this all out…” Lentus said, impressed. “Go ahead, kill me right now!” he demanded. “I'm not going to die a spectacle!”

“No!” Tsuki yelled as she stepped backward, sheathing her sword. “I'm not going to kill you. That's not what they would have wanted.”

“What?” exclaimed everyone, including the fallen king.

“I'm not going to kill you and tarnish their name. You will live the rest of your miserable life in the deepest, darkest part of the dungeon. That is what I have chosen,” Tsuki hissed at the man bound on the stone seat.

The head councilman nodded and crossed his arms. Finally, he said, “Guards! Take this farce away. Make sure he's locked up in a magical cell, tightly.”

A string of guards came from the wings when they were called; only once they had a hold of Lentus did Takagi let his binds go, his book falling into his hand. The guards swiftly took the fallen king away.

Tsuki sighed. “Did I do the right thing?” she asked herself.

She was startled by the feeling of a hand on her shoulder. It was Takagi, who then smiled and nodded at her. She was then enveloped by Kiriuk's arms, who picked her up and hugged her.

“Look at my sister!” he exclaimed. “She's so awesome and wise!”

The two of them made her laugh. The sense of being home returned to her, and she started crying. Kiriuk quickly set her down and asked what was wrong.

“I'm home… I'm finally home,” she said through her tears.

Chapter Ten

Homecoming

IT HAD BEEN a few weeks before everything had calmed down. Everyone in the land now knew of the treachery that Lentus had done and that Tsuki would correct everything. She had a long road ahead of her, but she would be okay with her friends by her side. She even sent for Willianna in Heltavin.

As soon as Tsuki saw her best friend, she got off her throne and ran to meet her. Both girls embraced each other tightly, thinking they would never see each other again. Willianna started to cry when she recounted receiving Tsuki's letter. Willianna then stopped and turned to look at a figure wearing a very wide and very ridiculous-looking hat. Tsuki continued crying as she saw who the hatted figure was.

"Alistain!" Tsuki cried out and ran to her love.

He took off his hat and hugged Tsuki tightly. "Oh, how I've missed you."

Tears filled Tsuki's eyes as she said, "I missed you too." Tsuki then impulsively kissed Alistain, who returned the kiss.

After a long while, Willianna cleared her throat, bringing the lovers back to reality. She then explained that as she was leaving for the Urufian capital, she was approached by Alistain and a strange man who matched Whitiker's description.

“But how? I thought you died that night.” Tsuki asked, puzzled.

Alistain retold the story of his fight with Whitiker and how he formed a blood pact with the man. “Whitiker is letting me live, but I cannot drink from humans anymore. Which is sad since there’s no sweeter taste than human blood, but I will live. He allowed me to come here and be with you while he finds a use for me. I'm not sure when that will be, so I will make the most of the time I have. He did say that he saw a spark in my eye while fighting, and that’s what made him decide to let me live. I believe the spark he saw was my love for you, Tsuki,” commented Alistain.

Takagi was now back as the head of the servants and court wizard for Tsuki. Kiriuk was made the head of the guard and was in charge of the local military. Tsuki recalled most of the Urufian troops from the front lines and her cousin, Clarent, and sent diplomats to the nations that had been taken over by the massive army of Urufu. This had all happened before Tsuki had been crowned. And, after all that was out of the way, things finally started to fall into place.

Tsuki was now paying her weekly visit to the graves of her parents. On this visit, she was kneeling, her eyes closed and hands clasped together.

"Mother. Father. I hope I have done you proud. I never could have dreamed of the mess he made. I will right his wrongs and make our nation, no, our world a better place." Tsuki said solemnly.

After she said what she had to say, Tsuki stood up and brushed herself off. As she did, she looked at Takagi, who stood beside her quietly. They nodded to each other and turned to leave the graveyard.

As they walked down a familiar path, Takagi turned to Tsuki and said, "Are you ready, my lady? It's time for you to find your spirit power."

"I've been thirteen years ready," Tsuki spoke with a timid smile.

"It's okay to be nervous; there will be many people," Takagi offered.

Tsuki sighed. He saw right through her tough act. "It's just that I've never been in front of so many people."

Takagi placed a hand on her shoulder. "I know it will take some getting used to. But you will always have me to guide you; do not fret."

"Thank you, Teacher," Tsuki said, smiling softly, "I think I'm ready."

"Good," was all Takagi said, and for the rest of the walk, they fell silent, each of them thinking and contemplating what would be Tsuki's guardian. Tsuki hoped she would be like her father, who had the power of an honorable stag, but she wouldn't discount her mother's dove power.

"Did they find him?" Tsuki asked quietly.

"Yes," Takagi replied. "He is being brought here from a faraway village. He and his family. I still do not understand why you want the man who killed your parents here."

"I have my reasons," Tsuki commented, smiling at her friend.

They came to a clearing with a giant lake and crystal-clear waters. It was so clear that one could see through all the way to the bottom and see all the fish in the lake. Several people were surrounding the lake. Most of them were commoners who came to watch this prestigious ceremony.

As Tsuki neared the lake's edge, she saw Alistain, Kiriuk, and Willianna standing nearby. Tsuki smiled at them with both excitement and nervousness. She was afraid she would get something disappointing but knew in her heart that it would fit her well.

The head councilman stepped forward out of the crowd, smiling at Tsuki. As he approached, he whispered to Tsuki, "Are you ready, child?"

Tsuki nodded, took a deep breath, and closed her eyes to focus.

"Now, walk into the water," instructed the councilman. "Only stop when you are chest-deep. Make sure the water covers your heart."

“Okay,” Tsuki replied. She opened her eyes and started walking forward. As she neared the water's edge, Tsuki took a hesitant step but powered through her nerves and walked into the water. The crisp water was surprisingly chilly for the warm afternoon. It was so frigid it sent a shiver up Tsuki’s spine. As the water level neared her chest, Tsuki saw something in the water. As she got deeper, it became more clear. It was a blue moon. It was distinct and apparent, but Tsuki still looked above her to the sky, only to see nothing but clouds and the tops of trees.

A wolf howled as she looked back down to take a second look at the water. It was so shockingly loud that everyone looked to see where it was coming from. Across the lake was the wolf. As Tsuki locked eyes with it, she noticed something. The wolf had the same golden eyes as the man who had saved her long ago.

Tsuki’s train of thought was broken by the councilman calling her, “My lady? Is everything alright?“

Tsuki blinked, and the wolf was gone. She took a breath and nodded, “Yes!” She slowly returned to the councilman, and several servants came to her, handing her towels and things to dry her off. Some even tried to help dry her, but Tsuki brushed them off. She took one of the towels and thanked the servants, who stopped their fussing to let her walk to the councilman.

As she reached the head councilman, she had a confused look on her face. “I only saw… the moon?” Tsuki said, puzzled.

"As did I," nodded the head councilman. "This must be a sign of the changing times. Good news, good news," the councilman said, turning to the crowd eagerly awaiting the announcement of Tsuki's guardian. He raised his hands, and the crowd grew still. He took a deep breath and nodded slowly. "So the legend is true," he whispered to himself.

Chapter Eleven

The Nightmare

A YEAR AFTER being crowned queen, Tsuki made strides to return her country to its former glory. She had already made treaties with all but one nation that Urufu had attacked unjustly. The economy was growing, and more jobs were being created to restore Urufu to what it had been before her uncle's reign of tyranny.

Tsuki had the man who had assassinated her parents and attempted to end her life brought before her. Standing in the throne room, he never looked Tsuki in the eye, ashamed of what he did.

"Your Majesty, I know there is nothing I can do to redeem myself. I have done something unspeakable to you and this country," the man said as he prostrated himself before Tsuki sitting on the throne.

Tsuki raised her hand, quieting the murmuring of those watching on, "If I remember correctly, in your attack, you said someone would hurt your family if you didn't kill my parents and myself. Who was this person?"

"I-it was the traitor Lentus, Your Majesty. I was an assassin in the Urufian military when he approached me," the man shivered as he recounted the meeting, "he threatened me with the death of my family and endless torture if I failed."

"Sounds about right," Tsuki muttered to herself. "Did you know any of his conspirators?"

Nodding furiously, the man started listing off several Urufian military leaders, a few well-known merchants in Urufu, and many affluent families. Tsuki motioned for the nearby scribe to write down the names of those Lentus trusted. After listing off everyone he knew with ties to the usurper, the man bowed, exhausted.

"Thank you for the information," Tsuki said as she waved the scribe away and turned back to the now crumpled man. "I have made my decision. While yes, you did something horrible, you were forced to do it. My decree is that you will hunt down these people and bring them back however possible. Your family will work in the castle as servants until you complete your task. Then you are to leave my country and never return."

The man was agape with surprise. "Thank you, Your Majesty, thank you."

Now that she was queen, she was trying to set things right, just like her parents would have done. The only hiccup was the last nation fighting peace with Urufu for generations: the country of Heltavin.

The country of Heltavin, known as the land of vampires, constantly fought with Urufu because the leaders wanted the magic from Mount Tsukismo. But

Tsuki was determined to have peace between the countries. Most of the vampires in the continent lived in Heltavin because of the dense trees, and even then, most preferred to travel at dusk or by night. There were whispers that the imperial line was composed of vampires. However, these were just rumors, as reliable information about Heltavin and its empire was hard to come by.

Tsuki often tossed and turned in her sleep as she dreamed. Well, it was more than a dream; it was a memory. It was when she was trapped and had the evil man, Dr. Gruten, conducting what he called research on her.

In her dream, Tsuki was tied to that rusty and cold slab of metal. She tried to get free, but she was tied tightly by her hands, feet, and neck.

But this night, everything was more real, more clear. In a rush, many ugly and mean-looking men dressed in brown or black entered the room. They surrounded her, so she could only see them and the bright white light fixture above her. It hurt her eyes to look up at the light, so all she had to look at were these horrible, leering men.

Suddenly, someone burst in from across the room. The sea of men parted for him. He was a short man with a facemask, so she wasn't sure who it was. This person was wearing pure white with black elbow gloves on. When she saw the gloves and looked back at the bespectacled, pale face, she knew it was Dr. Gruten even though she could not see his whole face.

Realizing who it was made her shiver and try to get free again. She struggled harder as the crowd of men laughed.

"Look at her."

"She thinks she can get away."

"She can't stop this."

They chanted these things repeatedly as Dr. Gruten walked toward the slab's head. As he walked, he took one of his gloved hands and skimmed his fingertips from Tsuki's foot all the way to her navel. Tsuki shivered and squirmed as he did so. She never wanted to be touched by that man ever again.

He stopped walking around halfway to the top of the slab, and when he stopped, he took his hand off Tsuki. That's when everyone in the room went quiet. Tsuki couldn't hear anything, not even the sound of someone breathing or her own breath or heartbeat. It was eerie.

As Tsuki looked around, Dr. Gruten pulled a scalpel from behind his back and raised it above his head with an evil smirk of glee on his face.

When she saw it, Tsuki froze; she quit struggling, and all the blood drained from her face.

"Now," Dr. Gruten announced behind his surgical mask, "you're all mine." As he finished his sentence, he took the scalpel and slammed it downward, knife end first into her stomach.

In a split second, Tsuki bolted upward in bed, awake from her nightmare. She screamed in terror and clutched her stomach. As she stopped screaming, she heard someone running from another room. It was Alistain. He rushed to her side to comfort her.

"Shhh. Shhh. I'm here; nothing can hurt you now." Alistain cooed as he wrapped his arms around Tsuki, rocking her back and forth.

"He was going to cut me open again," Tsuki wept into her lover's chest.

"He won't do that. He's gone, remember?" Alistain reassured her.

"I know. I know." Tsuki whimpered as she stifled a sob. "But it felt so real. Can- can you stay with me to make sure he doesn't come back?" she asked, looking up and meeting Alistain's deep red eyes.

"I'll do anything for you," he said softly, kissing her forehead. "Go ahead and sleep, my love. I will always be here."

With a knowing smile, Tsuki cuddled into Alistain and slowly returned to her slumber.

The following morning, she met with several Urufian leaders in the castle war room to discuss the problems that they were having with the Heltavin leader.

"They seem unreasonable!" Tsuki exclaimed as she sat at the head of the long war table. She leaned her head into her hands as her elbows rested on it. Scattered in front of her were many papers and reports.

The war room was decorated in an extravagant blue and silver theme. Even the glass of the enormous windows was etched with silver and hints of blue.

She was talking with the head of her armed forces, her cousin Clarent. He was dressed in full military garb, dress blues with gold shoulder pads similar to the ones her father used to wear for meetings and special occasions. He looked more like Tsuki's uncle than anything else. Their faces were very similar, but Clarent looked much younger and stockier. The similarity made her uneasy even though he denounced his father and swore loyalty to Urufu and its new queen quickly, stating that Lentus had never been a good father and was abusive to him and his mother. Clarent was the general of the Urufian army and loved its people. Tsuki knew that. That's why he was here.

"I know, Your Majesty, but their ruler, Emperor Klage, is a powerful tyrant. He has made his entire political platform fighting against us," Clarent stated as he walked around the table.

"Clarent," Tsuki sighed, "you know I don't like being called Your Majesty. It's Tsuki when we are in closed meetings like this."

Takagi, who was also in the room sitting next to Tsuki, sighed. He wore his long blue hair in a loose ponytail and his usual blue shirt with a blue coat and striped blue pants. He lifted his round glasses and pinched his nose at its bridge. He was a very wise and great tactician, which is why he was Tsuki's advisor.

"I apologize to you, Your Majesty, but I can't do that." Clarent chuckled.

"You know you can't make people change, sis," said Kiriuk. He was also wearing his usual long silver hair in a ponytail because he had just come from training the new recruits to become guards, and his silver wolf ears poked out from his hair. There had been an increase in people wanting to join the guard and army after Tsuki took the throne. Now that he had accepted the responsibility of being the head guard of the palace, he had grown a little. While he was still his same old goofy self, Kiriuk had matured in his actions. He wore his normal garb: a dark gray kimono shirt, pants with a blue trim, and a dark gray coat.

Kiriuk walked over to Clarent and started talking about wartime strategies and what it was like to fight in such a large group. “How intense is it on the battlefield?”

Clarent sighed, “Well, it's very chaotic. There is no way of knowing where the wall of killing begins and ends.”

“Wow!” Kiriuk exclaimed, patting Clarent hard on the shoulder, making the older man wince in pain.

“Yeah, it’s completely different from fighting in groups. You have to focus on keeping yourself alive instead of working as a team,” Tsuki’s cousin commented, shrugging. He looked at Tsuki with pleading eyes, almost asking for help from the endless questions from the energetic wolfman. Clarent had always been a quiet kid growing up, using his silence to analyze situations.

Suddenly, Takagi pulled his hand away from his face and straightened. "I've got an idea!" He exclaimed with excitement.

The room was silent again, with all eyes on the blue-haired man.

"What if we sent a diplomatic party down the old abandoned back roads." Takagi stated as he stood from his chair. He pointed to several places in Heltavin on the map of the world. "That way, we could sneak into Heltavin and get to the capital with limited effort, talk face-to-face with Emperor Klage, and see why he never responds to our letters!"

"That's a perfect idea, Takagi!" Tsuki called out with bubbling excitement. "We should talk to the council immediately and have us leave as soon as they approve this venture. This might be our chance to create peace!"

Takagi shook his head, walked over to Tsuki, and placed a hand over hers. "There is no 'we' or 'us,' Your Majesty. You're a queen now. You're too important. We can't afford for you to get hurt."

"But if the queen of the warring nation shows up on Heltavin's doorstep, they must take us seriously. At least that's what mom would have done." Tsuki huffed, crossing her arms.

"Yes, but Aunt Kusay made peace from a letter and a well-worded treaty, not by running up to their door." Clarent mimed as he talked since he had become deaf in one ear after a blow to his head in a recent battle, "Knock and say 'hello, might you share a spot of tea while we talk peace?'" He spoke in a high-pitched voice, mocking Tsuki.

"Yes, but they've denied all our written attempts to contact them or set up a meeting." Kiriuk whined.

"Right? We have to go in person!" Tsuki vocalized as she slammed her hand onto the war table.

"There is no 'we,' you are staying here." Takagi said sternly.

"Fine." Tsuki whined, "I know it's no use arguing with you."

"Good!" Takagi triumphantly nodded, “it seems you've finally taken to my teachings.”

That night, Takagi talked to the council about the venture to the capital of Heltavin. Thankfully, the councilmen were also upset with the lack of contact with Emperor Klage. The only additive to the plan was to have ambassadors go to Heltavin. The party would consist of one of the best warriors of Urufu and one of the greatest minds. So naturally, Kiriuk would go as a representative of their army, and Takagi would be chosen to represent the royal family. Also, Count Alistain and Tsuki's friend Willianna would be the ambassadors. Alistain was chosen for his knowledge of how the political system worked in Heltavin. Willianna went because of the ability to connect with others and gather information. And thus, the group was complete. Or so they thought.

While Alistain was getting ready for the journey, Tsuki pretended to sleep. Once he was out of the room, she quickly jumped out of bed to gather her things for the journey. She was already wearing her travel clothes: a dark gray kimono shirt with dark green trim, black pants, and her usual deep blue coat with red fur around the trim. Although she wanted to take it with her on the journey, she had decided to keep her father’s sword in the treasury vault for safekeeping. That way, she was less likely to be noticed as queen.

She had planned to hide in the cart the group took for supplies and things on their journey. Most of the group would be on horseback.

Early in the morning, Tsuki slipped out of her window and climbed down the outer wall. She was careful to not be seen as she approached the cart. Tsuki quickly dived into it and settled under the tarp, where all the supplies were. Her position wasn't the most comfortable, but it hid her well.

It wasn't long before she heard familiar voices approaching. It was Takagi and Alistain, but she heard more footsteps than just the two men. They were talking about their preparations and if they were ready to leave.

"So, how did Tsuki take you leaving her behind?" Takagi asked Alistain. Takagi was wearing his normal attire only with his hair let down.

"She wasn't happy and went straight to bed after her supper. Sulking, no doubt. I tried to have her promise me she wouldn’t follow us. But she was sleeping when I left our room." Alistain said as he got onto his horse.

Takagi agreed with Alistain and got on the cart to drive it. Tsuki then saw Willianna pass the cart. She was wearing her traveling clothes of a tan tube top with the symbol of the western country of Tepli, her birthplace, and her usual shorts with a scarf hanging down to her knee. She had gotten a little darker in skin tone from her usual olive-like color because she was tasked with leading a group of people from the couriers to address the major problems of the Urufian castle town. Her work kept her outside most of the time. She had climbed onto the cart, which left Kiriuk on the other horse.

A few hours of sleepy silence among the group left Tsuki tense that they might find her at any moment as they went. She could see both Takagi and Willianna; well, part of them, at least. All she could hear was the clopping of the horses' hooves and the cart rattling. Her body ached as she became stiff with anticipation. She had never gone against Takagi's orders with this severity before. Sure, she had disobeyed him a few times, but not this outright. Tsuki knew she would get scolded, but she didn't know if he would send her back. She hoped not. As Tsuki thought about these things, she closed her eyes and drifted off to sleep.

Chapter Twelve

Unwanted Guests

IT WAS LATE in the day when Tsuki awoke. She knew it was late because of the colors in the sky when she peeked out from underneath the tarp where she was hiding. Tsuki could feel the cool air of the evening start to blow. She knew they had gone a long distance because she was stiff from being in that position for a long time.

Soon, the cart stopped in a tiny clearing at the side of the road, probably because it was getting dark.

"Let us set up camp. No need to get ahead of ourselves. We have plenty of time to go slow." Takagi announced. The rest of the group verbally agreed with him.

With her wolf-like hearing, Tsuki heard someone get off their horse. She assumed it was Kiriuk as he was complaining about being on a horse for the entire day while she was awake.

"My legs hurt so much. Why do I have to ride a horse again?" Kiriuk moaned.

"You will get used to it." Alistain commented as he got off his horse.

"Speaking of getting used to something, Alistain." Willianna said nonchalantly. "How can you go into the sunlight like this since you are a vampire? Is it some mystical super vampire magic since you're so old?"

Alistain chuckled at Willianna's words, making him smile so big he showed his fangs. "Well, first off, thank you for calling me a super vampire; it's very flattering. And secondly, since I have drank the blood of those who turned me, I can be out in the sun. I have done something for Tsuki so she can be as powerful, if not more so, than me. But I cannot travel long distances without this wide-brimmed hat." Alistain told her. He was wearing a hat that looked like that of a rancher or cattle driver. "It helps shade me from the sun, just in case. Also, I get hotter faster because I do not sweat. So I have to drink lots of water. It has a bit of blood in it to keep me satisfied." He motioned to the large canteen on his hip.

As Willianna listened, she turned to grab something out of the cart. She pulled away the tarp Tsuki was hiding under. The older girl blindly reached for what she was looking for, not glancing down at the tarp as she lifted it. She searched around, patting things when she touched Tsuki's hair.

Willianna jumped back in shock, not expecting something so soft. She yelped and looked down in surprise. "Tsuki?!" She fell backward in surprise at seeing her friend there and flailed as she hit the ground with a thud.

Takagi whipped around in his seat and yanked the tarp off the cart. There was a beat of silence as everyone stared into the cart, including Willianna, who had quickly returned to her feet.

Tsuki sat up and tentatively looked at Takagi. He was red in the face, looking like he might explode. And that is exactly what he did as he started to yell at Tsuki.

"Tsuki, I mean, Your Majesty?! What the hells are you doing here?" Takagi screamed as he flailed his arms in frustration. "You aren't supposed to be here! You're supposed to be safe at the castle, leading the country. But no... you had to sneak into the cart and try to come with us!"

At this point, Alistain was also yelling at Tsuki. "Why are you here? You lied to me! You said you would stay at the castle where you are supposed to be!"

Kiriuk, on the other hand, was bouncing up and down with excitement, clapping. "Big sis is coming with us! Big sis is coming with us!"

Willianna stood still in shock and looked from person to person, trying to get a read on the situation. "Wha... wha?" Was all she could say.

As everyone stopped their yelling of either anger or excitement to catch their breath, Tsuki looked down at her crossed legs and twiddled her thumbs nervously.

Takagi continued his tirade after a beat of silence, only with a softer rage this time. "How dare you go against me. I am your advisor and have more experience with things like this than you will ever have. As soon as dawn breaks, one of us will ride with you back to the castle, and you will stay there!"

"No! I am the ruler!!" Tsuki yelled as she looked up at Takagi. Everyone got still and looked at her in stunned silence. She rarely pulled the power of being Queen and never on Takagi. "Like I said yesterday during the meeting, they are more likely to take us seriously if you have me there. They might even agree to peace! You can't send me back now! Besides, I have Clarent and your understudy handling everything. I left explicit instructions."

While Tsuki yelled her argument, Takagi calmly took things out of the cart and handed them to Kiriuk and Willianna as if his mind were made up, and the conversation was over.

"She does have a point, wizard." Alistain said as Takagi approached him with tent supplies in his arms. "The Heltavin leaders will take us more seriously if we have her. As much as I want to keep her safe, I feel she is safer with us than anywhere else."

"Oh, don't go soft on me now, man!" Takagi protested.

It was now three against one with Tsuki. Alistain and Kiriuk were on one side, and Takagi was all by himself on the other. Willianna was still trying to make out the situation due to her surprise.

"Fine, I see how it is." Takagi grumbled as he turned away from Alistain and started to pitch the tent himself. "We are getting nowhere while yelling at each other. Let us set up camp and talk about this over dinner."

Everyone, including Tsuki, agreed to this short-term plan. But as the grumpy wizard was getting things out of the cart, Tsuki and Kiriuk heard something in the brush nearby with their keen hearing.

Out of nowhere, an arrow flew towards Takagi's head. Tsuki pushed herself out of the cart with lightning-like reflexes and tackled Takagi, making the arrow miss his head by a few centimeters. As they tumbled, a band of gross-looking Heltavin bandits rushed the group.

"But we're not even near the border! They have some nerve attacking this close to the castle!" Willianna exclaimed as she got out her slingshot.

Alistain drew his sword, and Kiriuk jumped to grab his spear attached to his saddle.

As Kiriuk was the closest to the wizard and Tsuki, he stood to defend them against two large men, preventing him from making the first strike. Kiriuk got in between the two bandits, and Tsuki and Takagi evaded their attacks. At the same time, Kiriuk blocked them with his spear.

Alistain made quick work of another bandit who was wielding a sword. By using his speed to get behind the dirty man, Alistain used his own sword to run him clean through with his sharp blade. The bandit then fell to his knees as Alistain kicked him off the blade.

Willianna used her slingshot to stun the archer and ran up to him quickly, dodging the others. She swiftly dispatched the archer with a clean cut to his throat with the small knife that she kept hidden underneath her scarf at her hip.

Willianna put away her short blade and turned to aim her slingshot at the assailants who were attacking Kiriuk. She rapidly let loose two shots at them. Sadly, all that did was make them angry, causing them to turn and charge towards her.

This allowed Kiriuk to attack the two large men. He slashed their legs, making them fall as they ran. He then stabbed them between the ribs, killing them instantly.

As the dust of the battle settled, Tsuki lifted herself off of Takagi. "Are you alright? I was afraid I wouldn't make it in time."

Takagi chuckled. "I'm the one who should be asking that. You put yourself in danger to save me. Thank you, little one." The wizard said the last sentence softly as he kissed Tsuki's forehead.

Takagi hadn't called Tsuki "little one" in public for quite some time. Such a gesture was usually used as an endearment as she grew up, praising Tsuki for following his guidance and making good decisions.

"Are you alright, my love?" Alistain called out as he rushed to Tsuki's side and helped her off Takagi.

"We are both fine, thanks for asking." Takagi muttered under his breath.

"I saved Takagi from the archer. So see! I can be useful on this journey, and now you owe me, Takagi." Tsuki gloated.

The wizard sighed with a smile. "I guess I do owe you. Fine. You can stay, but only if you keep a low profile. Okay?"

"Okay!" Tsuki cried out in triumph.

Chapter Thirteen

A Little Cottage

AS TSUKI WOKE on their third day of traveling, she yawned and stretched, her wolf ears twitching as she did so. She ensured her partner did not wake up, as Alistain was still sleeping. He had stayed up all night before they had left and was awake the full extent of their days of travel. He was also trying to get used to sleeping at night instead of the day like most vampires. This change made him very tired, so Tsuki let him sleep a little longer.

After the first day, when the bandits had attacked the group, everything seemed to settle down. The group's banter had lightened up; even Takagi wasn't so stiff. He had even called Tsuki by her name instead of Your Majesty, which made Tsuki very happy. She had never liked the formalities of titles; she felt they separated the person from their duties.

After laying on her bedroll for a while, listening to the morning birds and the wind softly blowing through the trees, Tsuki decided she had better get up and dressed. She wore normal traveling clothes and fastened her boots as she readied for the day.

As she put on her boots, Tsuki heard someone humming outside the tent. Once she finished lacing her boots, Tsuki opened the tent entrance and was hit by the smell of something wonderful cooking over the fire in the center of camp.

Their camp was small, with only three tents and a small fire. The sleeping arrangements weren't ideal as they hadn't expected a fifth person. So, two tents were always full while one person stood watch. Takagi and Kiriuk stayed in one tent because they had grown accustomed to sleeping like this since their journey to find Tsuki took years. Tsuki and Alistain shared a tent, of course, which left Willianna in her own tent. This was fine with the others because Willianna tended to snore at night, not so much that it would bother others in another tent. However, staying with her in a tent would prove sleepless.

As for where they were, the group had found an outcropping in the woods next to the road. That way, they were hidden from view of anyone on the road. Their mission was still secret, with only a select few who knew of their plans, so they needed to stay out of sight or at least as inconspicuous as possible.

Tsuki sat next to the fire, and Takagi joined her. He handed her a metal cup filled with hot, black coffee. He knew exactly what she needed to wake up.

"How did you sleep, my dear?" Takagi asked as he stirred a pot hanging above the fire.

Now that she could see what was in it, Tsuki recognized the fabulous smell of oatmeal. "I slept fine. I had trouble falling asleep after my shift, but otherwise, I'm well rested." Tsuki replied after taking a sip of the warm liquid. She had never gone without a cup of morning coffee for at least two years. And that was thanks to Takagi and his same habit.

Soon, everyone else poured sleepily out of their tents, yawning and stretching. All except Alistain. He was still fast asleep when Willianna took the cooking and eating utensils to wash in a nearby stream.

"When will your man ever get up in a timely manner?" Willianna quipped at Tsuki jokingly as she gathered the dishes.

"When you stop being so sassy." Tsuki snarked back, handing her plate to her friend.

"You know that's in my blood. I get it from my mom, and so do you." Willianna laughed as she walked off to clean the dishes.

Tsuki went into their tent and woke Alistain with a kiss on the cheek. The group started to take down the camp and load everything into the cart. Once Willianna returned with clean dishes, Alistain and Kiriuk checked their horses and put their saddles on to get ready to leave. Tsuki was checking the cart horses when Willianna came up beside her, holding a map of Urufu and Heltavin with a marked trail the group was taking.

"Umm. Hey, boss lady?" The older girl asked softly.

"What is it?" Tsuki asked in response.

Willianna tilted her head to the side and looked at the map harder. "It shows here that we will be passing through a village. I thought we were supposed to be traveling in secret."

"Umm. Uhhh?" Tsuki stuttered as she looked around for Takagi.

"Well, we are young ones." Takagi said as he readied the cart horses. "We must pass through a tiny village to continue our journey and get more supplies. Thankfully, I know that this town is not militarized by our soldiers, so we have no worries about being outed."

"Fewf!" The girls sighed.

"We need to get going to make it there by noon." Alistain said. He was already on his horse, ready to travel.

"Right!" Everyone else cheered.

It didn't feel like a long ride until they reached the village Willianna was talking about. It was a quaint village with only a handful of houses and a well in the middle. As the group pulled in, children played with a dog, and women hung laundry on lines.

As they approached the village center, they heard someone shouting. "Damn it all! Why did she have to curse me like this?!"

A woman crossed to the courtyard near the well towards another woman. She was steaming mad and covered in a purple goo.

"I'm tired of every other pie I make exploding right in my face, Tatiana," said the goo-covered lady.

"I know, dearie, but it can't be helped." The other woman shrugged.

"I'm sorry, but what is the matter?" Willianna asked as she hopped off the cart.

Tsuki slid off Alistain's horse, walked up to the distressed lady, and handed her a towel from the cart.

"I've been cursed by that old witch outside of town!" The woman said as she cleaned her face off with the towel.

"Why?" Tsuki asked as the woman finished cleaning her face. She tried to return the towel to Tsuki, but the young girl declined it as it was clear the woman needed it more than Tsuki.

"Well," the other woman started as she finished hanging her laundry a few yards away from the well. "It seems that the old hag is in distress about something. But even those she called friends, she would curse if they knocked on her door. Now, mind you, these curses aren't horrible, just inconvenient."

"Inconvenient is a light way of stating it," said the angry woman. "She cursed me so that every other pie

I make explodes in my face, and she cursed my husband when he went to get to the bottom of this. Now he can't light a fire correctly."

Kiriuk huffed, "That does sound annoying."

"I say we check it out. There's no harm in doing so, right?" Tsuki said to Takagi, who nodded in response.

"Thank you for the information, young ladies. Now, where is this witch?" Takagi asked as he gave the two women a charming smile.

"Oh my! Well, she's just down that road and over the hill," said the other woman, blushing a little.

Tsuki and Willianna jumped back into their seats and encouraged everyone to get ready to leave. As they approached the hill, they spotted the small cottage with smoke billowing out of the chimney. Tsuki hopped off Alistain's horse again and ran to the door. She knocked with enthusiasm and thundered, "Hello? Is anyone home? I'm not from around here, and I need to ask you a few questions, please."

There was a long silence. Tsuki knocked again and repeated her phrase, louder this time. Then, from inside the cottage, floorboards were shuffling and creaking.

"I'm coming; no need to shout!" Yelled an elderly female voice from the other side of the door.

The door to the cottage flung open, and a very angry, old, large woman stood hunched over. She had a cane raised in the air like a weapon. She then looked Tsuki and her group over and then smiled. "Hmm. A she-wolf and her band of merry men. How interesting. Come in! Come in!" said the elderly lady as she turned around and let the group inside.

The witch was large and gray-headed with hair down to her chin. She was wearing a light purple dress that complemented her purple eyes. She had a wrinkly face and waddled as she walked.

"Thank you," commented Tsuki as she entered the cottage.

The one-story building looked very much like a mad witch's hut on the inside. There were baubles everywhere, books stacked on top of each other, and potion bottles strung about the place. It was a mess. But it was a homey one.

"So whatcha need to ask little old me?" The witch asked.

"Well, to get right to it, we heard you were cursing everyone who comes here to check on you. Why is that?" Tsuki queried.

The witch sighed. "Well, ya see, these kids come up here every afternoon and throw rocks at my door. Sometimes they knock on my door and scare me when I open it," the witch said as she sat down in an ancient rocking chair that squeaked as she sat and rocked. "I'm a hundred and six! I think I deserve a little peace and quiet."

"So those little brats are terrorizing you? Then why do you curse the adults?" Takagi asked.

"I go into town every Thursday. I don't know why they are suddenly checking in on me. I can take care of myself just fine. Have done it just fine for ninety years. Those older folks should have stopped the kids from scaring me!" The old witch exclaimed as she waved her cane around wildly.

"Maybe they are just worried. I mean, it seems like there are a lot of people in that village who care about you. Maybe they didn't know about the kids," Willianna said, taking a step forward.

"You're right, you're right. They have been nice to me in my old age. They rarely ask me for potions and spells to heal them; in return, they give me many things. And I am good friends with a lot of them. Maybe I was too harsh to attack the adults. But how can I know who's at my door if they don't announce themselves? That's what those rotten kids do when they scare me."

"Well, what if we teach those kids a lesson and make them apologize to you?" Tsuki offered, putting her hands on her hips.

"That would do just fine, youngin. You do that, and I'll even promise to lift all the curses I've done on the villagers."

"Wonderful!" Tsuki said excitedly.

The group quickly left the cottage with the old witch behind them. That's when they started to form their game plan to search for the kids of the small village.

They agreed that splitting up would be the best way to find them. Tsuki and Takagi would search one half of the village, and Alistain, Kiriuk, and Willianna would search the other half. Once they got to the center of the village, they split up. It took a while before Tsuki and Takagi came upon a group of four children torturing a little frog trying to run away. That was when they knew that they had the right group of children. As Tsuki and the wizard approached the kids, the boys looked up, saw the two strangers, and ran away.

"Wait, we just want to talk!" Tsuki yelled as she and Takagi ran after the kids.

Because of their longer legs and training, Takagi and Tsuki soon cornered the children.

"We weren't doin' anything wrong."

"We were just playing."

"Yeah! Nothing wrong." The boys yelled in protest.

"You know," Takagi said, a little out of breath, "If you run away from the scene, that means you're guilty of something. Besides, who gave you the right to hurt an innocent frog like that? And definitely, no right to treat the witch like you do. Let me tell you something..." his nagging was cut off by Tsuki walking in front of him and kneeling down before the kids.

"You know what you are doing to that old woman is wrong, don't you? How would you like to be treated like you treated her?" Tsuki said calmly.

"I wouldn't like it." Said one of the boys after a beat of silence.

"Then don't you think you should stop?" Tsuki continued.

"Yeah, she's right. I had never thought of it like that. Besides, it's causing problems for our parents," said another boy.

"Let's go apologize! Then maybe we can have pie!" said a third boy.

"Yeah!" The kids said in unison.

Tsuki smiled as she stood and watched the kids run toward the witch's cottage. "Let's go find the others, hm?"

Takagi smiled softly, nodded, and fell behind Tsuki as she walked toward the center of town.

As the two approached the well, they saw their companions. Tsuki saw Willianna wave at them, and she waved back.

"We found them and talked to them." Takagi said, putting a hand on Tsuki's shoulder. "Or I should say Tsuki talked to them."

"Way to go, sis!" cried Kiriuk excitedly. "Now, let's go talk to that fat hag."

"Kiriuk!" Exclaimed Takagi as he bonked Kiriuk on the head.

"Ow! What?" Kiriuk said, rubbing his head.

It didn't take them long to reach the cottage again. This time, the four boys were knocking on the witch's door.

"Lady witch? We want to apologize," said one of the kids.

"Yeah!" said the rest.

Tsuki and her gang dismounted and walked up behind the kids.

"Hi, nice lady!" said another boy.

The door to the cottage flung open with the familiar scene of the old witch with her raised cane. She looked from Tsuki and her group down to the four boys twiddling their thumbs.

"Oh?" said the witch.

"Yeah, we are really sorry that we did all those mean things to you," stated the first boy.

"We wouldn't want anyone to do that to us, so we are stopping now," commented another.

"Can you forgive us and fix our parents, please?" asked a third.

"Well..." said the witch. "I guess I can forgive you. But only if you promise to never do anything like that to anyone else," she said as she leaned down, smiling at the children.

"Okay!" the boys yelled.

"We promise!" yelled the fourth boy as he put his hand out. The other boys stacked their hands on his and raised them triumphantly into the air. Then they ran back to the village, saying what fun things they might do next.

"Ah... maybe I'll have some peace and quiet now." The witch mumbled under her breath. She then turned to Tsuki. "Tell me, girl, are you and that boy both werewolves? It's rare to see two in one place."

"Well, actually, it's a long story, but I'm a wolf turned into a man," explained Kiriuk. "So I'm not an actual werewolf. But sis is!" he pointed at Tsuki.

"Now that's an interesting tale. Please come in; I want to hear more!" The witch said as she invited them in again. She flopped into her rocking chair, making it squeak.

"Well..." Kiriuk started hesitantly. "When I was a pup, my mom and I were separated during a big lightning storm. And so, I searched for food for the next few days."

The witch nodded as she listened. So did Alistain and Willianna, who had not yet heard this story.

"So I came upon a building of some sort." Kiriuk continued. "It looked huge to me, but I smelled something delicious. I had been without food for three days at that point, and I was scared. So I searched for a way to get into the building and found a stack of boxes I could climb up to a window. And at that window, there was a pie! So, naturally, I started eating it. But I guess the pie owner did not like that, and she ran at me with a wand. I fell off the boxes, and before I could hit the ground, I was in the form of a human boy."

"Oh my," Willianna said softly.

"So I ran deep into the woods and ran into a werewolf man who then raised me to be a man and fighter, and he raised Tsuki as well. That's why I call her sis." Kiriuk chuckled. "And the rest is history."

There was a short silence then the witch sucked in a shaky breath. "I remember," she said quietly.

"You remember?" Tsuki asked.

The witch nodded, "I remember because I was that witch who cursed you into a man. I was younger and more brash back then. I'm sorry I didn't think before I acted."

"It's quite alright. If you hadn't done what you did, I wouldn't be alive today," Kiriuk shrugged.

"Yes, but I stuck you in that body without giving you a choice. Ah!" The witch exclaimed as she got up from her chair. "I have something to fix that."

She waddled over to a desk covered in books and dug through the stuff there. "Aha! Found it!" She shuffled back toward the group and went toward Kiriuk. She held a blue necklace with a crescent-shaped white moon as the pendant. She tied it around Kiriuk's neck and smiled.

"Now, if you touch the crescent three times, you will become a wolf again. Your clothes will disappear until you touch it thrice and turn back human." The witch explained.

"You just had this lying around?" Willianna asked skeptically.

"Well, it's a reverse spell kind of necklace. So it should work how I described." The old witch laughed.

"I'm going to try it right now!" Kiriuk said excitedly. He ran out of the cottage, and his friends followed. He touched the pendant thrice, and a silver light shone from the crescent. The light was so bright the others had to look away. When they looked back at Kiriuk, he had become a gray wolf with the necklace around his neck. It was Kiriuk in his original form, just older!

He looked around and then looked at himself. He lifted his paws one at a time and placed them back on the ground. He then started to run around barking excitedly. Only Tsuki could understand him since she was a werewolf. “I'm a wolf! Yes! I'm a wolf again!" Kiriuk barked.

Tsuki turned back to the cottage door where the witch stood, leaning on her cane. "Thank you so much. You have no idea how much this means to him."

At that point, Kiriuk had become a man again with his usual ears and tail. He walked up to the witch and hugged her. "Thank you. I can finally be whole again."

The witch laughed and hugged Kiriuk back. But before she could even open her mouth to reply, someone else said something.

"What's all the commotion around here? I heard that a group of travelers talked with our witch?" An older gentleman said as he walked down the path towards the cottage.

"Ah! Kids, this is the village leader. Yes, they talked with me and have fixed my problem. Have those I have cursed come to me tomorrow, and I shall lift their plight." The old witch decried.

"Really?" The leader asked. "Well, that requires a reward! How about I let you travelers sleep in my inn for free with a free meal!"

"Yay!" The group cried and nodded.

As they said their goodbyes to the witch, Kiriuk hugged her again. They slept comfortably in the inn with full bellies as they had a feast dedicated to them, including a pie from a once angry woman.

Chapter Fourteen

More Problems

AFTER SEVERAL LONG days of travel, Tsuki sunk into a deep sleep one night. When she opened her eyes, she was standing in a long, dark hallway. She looked around to get her bearings, but she saw something strange. The walls and floor seemed like they were undulating with no rhythm. This made Tsuki stagger and struggle to balance. Her tail was flicking around, trying to help her stand up straight. As she started to find her footing, the echo of footsteps came from the blackness.

Tsuki looked towards the sound and saw two figures approaching her. She could not identify them from where they were, so she tried to find a familiar scent. There was a strong odor of death and metal.

As the figures moved closer, she saw something falling off the shorter one. It made a splat when it hit the ground. As they got closer and closer to Tsuki, it was apparent that they weren't normal humans. They were larger and warped.

She didn't like the situation one bit, so she tried to turn and run. As she moved to lift her leg, nothing happened. She looked down at her feet, and she had sunken down into the moving floor. She couldn't move her feet. That's when she started to panic. She struggled against her bonds with no success. Tsuki then looked up to see where the figures were. She screamed in horror.

It was Dr. Gruten and her uncle Lentus. But they looked wrong. Lentus was shifting like lightning, moving rapidly in an unnatural way. He was dressed in his regal clothes, which were dingy and falling apart. And the doctor looked like he had just been dug up from a grave. Mud was falling off of him, along with worms and maggots. His clothes were also deteriorating, and she could see bone where there was no clothing.

"Come here, my perfect little test subject. I want to play with you." Dr. Gruten said, even though his jaw was hanging like a thread.

"You'll never be like your parents. You'll fail your country," said Lentus, emphasizing every word. It made the words sting all the more.

"Wha- what? No!" Tsuki said defiantly.

The two monsters, as Tsuki would have called them, continued to walk toward her. She struggled against her stuck feet, only to fall over and catch herself with her hands.

"What kind of leader leaves her country for a silly adventure?" Lentus continued to berate her.

"Don't worry, it will only hurt a lot," Gruten laughed evilly.

They spat out every word as they walked closer and got bigger and bigger, taller than a house. This made Tsuki feel so small. She started to panic, her breath became shorter, and her head spun. Tsuki then looked up at the monsters, feeling nauseated because of their height and her spinning head.

Suddenly, they stopped walking a few meters before the stooped over Tsuki. She was still looking up at them. Then they raised a fist in the air and swung downwards quickly. Even though their size was huge, it didn't take long for their fists to come upon Tsuki.

She screamed and covered her head, waiting for the inevitable pain of being crushed. She could hear the wind parting as their fists came downward. Then everything went dark.

Tsuki awoke screaming and immediately scrunched into a ball and covered her head. Her scream was loud enough to wake her sleeping partner, Alistain. He bolted upright and grabbed his sword from beside him. He looked around and found Tsuki shivering in fear. She had stopped screaming and was sobbing now.

That's when Alistain realized she had a nightmare. She had suffered from them for years, but only in the past year had they gotten so bad she was having panic attacks without him there. She would hate to go to sleep and try to stay up with him all night, only to pass out a few hours later.

Alistain rushed over to Tsuki and picked her up in his arms. He rocked her, trying to get her to calm down. He stroked her hair and whispered to her, "It's ok. They can't hurt you now.”

There was a ruckus outside of their tent, and in burst Takagi. "Is she alright? What happened? Where are those who hurt her?" As he finished his frantic questions, he entered the tent and tripped hastily. He fell on the ground next to Alistain, face first as well.

"Alistain? Takagi?" Tsuki said quietly as she started to calm down and relax.

"She'll be fine, wizard. Just another nightmare." Alistain said calmly as he stifled a chuckle.

"Oh, thank the gods," Takagi said under his breath as he got up from his fall and dusted himself off.

"I don't want to go back to sleep after that," Tsuki said as she nuzzled Alistain's shoulder.

Takagi knelt down next to the couple and sighed. "It's fine. It's about time for everyone to get up anyway. So do not worry, little one." He smiled softly.

Tsuki looked up at him and sighed in relief. "Thank you."

After Takagi left the tent, Tsuki and Alistain dressed and prepared for the day. They sat in the tent for a while longer, trying to erase the nightmare from her mind.

That morning was just like usual, except everyone was quiet around Tsuki. All but Willianna. They had heard her scream and were tentative to ask about it. Willianna disregarded that and treated this morning like any other. She treated Tsuki like normal as well.

"So, miss wolf-brain. Would you like more eggs?" Willianna said as she took Tsuki's plate from her.

"No, I think I'm fine, miss thinks-that-shorts-are-good-traveling-clothes." Tsuki sassed back. She was thankful someone was trying to keep things like they used to. Willianna was perfect for that job. Willianna knew what Tsuki's nightmares were like since they had lived together for so long. The two women had quite a connection, almost knowing exactly what the other needed.

After a few quips back and forth between the two girls, everyone was in high spirits again and ready to move out. But before they were done loading the cart back up, Alistain walked over to Takagi.

"Takagi, we need to have a talk." Alistain said sternly, "In private."

Takagi looked at Alistain hesitantly. "Ok?"

The two men slipped unnoticed into the brush as everyone else was busy breaking down camp. Alistain and Takagi stopped a good ways away from the camp so that they knew no one with heightened hearing could catch anything.

"So what is this about?" asked Takagi, arms across his chest.

Alistain shifted his weight, trying to put his words delicately. "I've noticed that you've become very close to Tsuki. Calling her by her name and 'little one.' It doesn't sit right with me."

"Wait, are you jealous that I'm showing endearment towards someone I've known their whole life? This is ridiculous!" Takagi exclaimed, “I’ve always called her little one.”

"I'm not jealous. I'm just trying to confirm my suspicions." Alistain said calmly, trying to not have this conversation break into a fight.

"Suspicions of what?" Takagi countered, putting his hands on his hips.

"That you... well, there is no other way to put it. That you are in love with her."

"How... why... when did you?" Takagi stuttered, taken aback by Alistain's words. A blush graced Takagi’s cheeks.

"Please don't make this difficult by denying it. It was confirmed this morning when you were so ready to comfort her." Alistain said as he put a hand on Takagi's shoulder.

"Fine, I admit it. I am fond of Tsuki. But I know my place. I know that she will never love me back. So I will stay to the side and watch from afar. There is no need for you to be threatened by me." Takagi sighed as he extended a hand to Alistain.

Alistain took the hand and nodded, "Then we have an accord. We both look after her, but leave the intimate things to me."

"Agreed," Takagi said with a nod and a sad look.

As they went back to the camp in silence, they saw the rest of the group waiting. Seeing this made the two men know they had to quickly think of a cover story.

"So, what were you two doing while we were hard at work?" Kiriuk said as he crossed his arms in front of him.

"We were, uh..." Alistain started to say.

"I was checking how Alistain was faring with this increased sun intake. We needed someplace dark so I could ensure he wasn't sunburnt or anything like that." Takagi said smoothly. "He's fine for now, but I must check again in a few days."

Satisfying their curiosity with his explanation, the group began packing. After that was done, they set off for the Urufian-Heltavin border.

Soon, the hours were passing in comfortable silence for the group. That was until Kiriuk let his curiosity get the better of him. As soon as he opened his mouth, the group knew it would be awkward.

"So, sis. What was your nightmare about? You screamed loudly this morning, so I assumed you had another one." The young wolfman chirped. He meant well and never did well with silence.

"Kiriuk!" Willianna and Alistain yelled at the same time.

Takagi just buried his head in his hands and sighed. "Kiriuk, you can't just ask someone that."

"Why not? Maybe we could help with some of her worries." Kiriuk said in protest, holding his head high.

"It's fine, guys," Tsuki said as she chuckled. "I haven't talked with him about the nightmares, so he wouldn't know that I don't like talking about them."

"Really?" said Kiriuk in surprise. "If I had any idea they were that uncomfortable for you, I wouldn't have asked."

"See! Pure innocence," Tsuki said as she broadly gestured at Kiriuk.

"Oh my gods," Willianna said as she slammed her palm into her forehead, smacking loudly.

This sound made the rest of the group laugh. The lightheartedness of the conversation extended for a while until they reached their destination of the border. But what they saw was not what they were expecting.

As the group rode up to the border, they were greeted with a large fence of fallen trees stuck together and guarded by soldiers. From their uniforms, it was clear they were Heltavin soldiers. The crest on their chest was a bear holding a crossbow. The colors surrounding the bear were dark green and deep crimson. They were also wearing standard soldier garb of armor and a helmet. The Heltavin men also had either a sword or a spear.

Two soldiers were standing next to an opening in the fence line that created a checkpoint on the road the group was on. The gap was big enough for a cart to go through, but that was about it. The rest of the soldiers, at least three, were walking the perimeter of the fence.

Takagi stopped the group as soon as he could see the soldiers. He cursed under his breath and looked around.

"Why are we stopping? It's just a checkpoint." Willianna asked.

"We can't. They won't let us through since we are, or at least some of us are Urufian." Takagi explained.

"Who says that they won't let us through," Willianna said quizzically.

Tsuki then pointed to a sign hanging above the heads of the soldiers standing guard. The sign was written poorly in red paint; Tsuki hoped it was paint, at least. The sign said, "NO URUFIAN BLOOD MAY ENTER. ALL WILL BE CHECKED FOR PERMIT."

"What does that even mean?" Kiriuk whined. "I thought you said there wouldn't be anyone on these roads."

"There weren't supposed to be. But I guess they have upped their watch at the border because of the war," Takagi said as he covered his mouth with his hand, deep in thought. "In Heltavin, they would give you a permit to travel. I guess that permit would let you cross the border."

"That way, they keep track of who's coming in and out of the country," Alistain said, almost as if he was reading Takagi's train of thought. "So that way is out of the question. Any other ideas?"

"We could... go around," Tsuki said as she subtly pointed off the side of the road. There was an end to the log fence that made the border that no one else had seen. "It'll be hard for the cart, but we can make it through at night."

So, together, as a group, they decided to go with Tsuki's plan. They would camp in the middle of the forest surrounding the road so no one would see them and wait for night. They also ensured that they gave the soldiers a wide berth when they left in the middle of the night.

As they waited for nightfall, the group ate and rested. That way, they would be ready to move out whenever it got dark. Kiriuk took it upon himself to change into his wolf form and scout out a good path the cart could follow. He also watched for any openings in the rounds of the guards so they weren't going in blind.

While the others were waiting, they developed a few signals to communicate with Kiriuk, who would lead in his wolf form. He would direct the cart with Alistain driving, and Tsuki and Willianna would bring up the rear.

Willianna would ride Kiriuk's horse so they didn't have it tied to the cart. The signals were a short bark for a stop, a growl for slower, and a short howl for faster, meaning someone was coming.

When nightfall finally came, everyone pitched in, quickly and quietly packing up the camp. They snuffed the fire so the guards couldn't see the glow through the trees. The group grew silent so as not to give away their position.

As they mounted up and Kiriuk turned into a wolf again, it was pitch black around them. They were thankful that most of the group had some sort of night vision. Kiriuk, with his wolf sight; Takagi, with his hawk-like sight and his magic; Tsuki and Alistain, with their vampire sight, all had no trouble in the dark. Sadly, Willianna couldn't see in the dark, so she stuck close to Alistain and Tsuki as she rode.

They went normally, with Takagi following Kiriuk as he trotted along a path he planned out earlier. Thankfully, this secret path had a few bumps that made the cart unsteady. There were only a handful of spots when Takagi had to call Kiriuk back with a whistle to find another way.

As they slowly progressed toward the edge of the fence, they could see the light from the guard's torches. They could also hear the clanking from their armor. This would make it easier, but they still needed to be cautious about when they would go and when they stopped.

When they were nearly upon the fence, Kiriuk realized they had made it too close to where the patrol was. And there was another big problem. Kiriuk then let out a short bark to stop the group. He talked to Tsuki about the situation.

"There's a steep slope that the cart might have trouble getting up," Tsuki whispered to Takagi.

"We have to try!" Takagi whispered back.

With a nod, Kiriuk led them to the slope. He waited until there was a break in the patrol and ran up the slope himself. He made it up easily. As did Alistain and Willianna. The cart horses had a little trouble, but the cart had the most difficulty. As the horses pulling it tried their best, they could not get the cart over the ridge. They knew they were running out of time as they saw a torch coming closer and closer.

Alistain hopped off his horse and ran behind the cart. He began pushing it as hard as he could. He pushed for a while, but the cart barely budged. So, Tsuki, seeing little progress being made, jumped off the horse and handed the reins to Willianna, who was preparing a shot from her slingshot towards the unsuspecting guard. Kiriuk let out a howl, signaling for them to move faster. Tsuki ran next to Alistain and pushed. Suddenly, the cart lurched over the rim it was stuck on, leaving the lovers in the dust and falling forward. The two scrambled to get onto their horse.

Unfortunately, all their rushing made a noise that the guard heard. "Huh?" He said as he slowly got closer.

If they didn't act fast, he would notice the cart, and their cover would be blown. Takagi continued to move the cart as Kiriuk ran up to the man.

"Wha! A wolf!" he said as he tried to draw his sword.

Kiriuk growled at the man. He was trying to distract the guard from looking into the distance and seeing the cart roll away. Kiriuk circled the guard and made him turn away from where the cart was.

"Damn wolf, get outta here!" said the guard. The guard waved the torch before him, trying to scare Kiriuk off.

Kiriuk growled again as the cart got further and further from the guard. Suddenly, a loud whistle came from Takagi. That was the signal for the all clear.

"Hiyah, hiyah!" Yelled the guard, still waving the torch.

Kiriuk stopped and looked toward the cart, barely seeing it; he knew they were safe. So he turned and ran toward his companions, only looking back once to the guard, making sure he didn't follow. He quickly caught up to his friends and barked a hello at them.

"Holy... don’t scare me like that. You came out of nowhere." Willianna said softly.

"You hurt?" Takagi asked as he twisted in his seat to look at his friend.

Kiriuk barked twice.

"He says no. And asks how much further." Tsuki translated.

Takagi chuckled and responded, "Not much further. Do you mind looking for a clearing friend?"

Kiriuk barked again and ran ahead of the group. He soon disappeared into the trees.

Takagi, feeling they should be safe from being spotted by now, stopped the cart. After a few moments, Kiriuk returned with a smile on his face.

"Looks like he found us a spot," Willianna said happily, forgetting they needed to be quiet a little longer. She was shushed by Alistain and Takagi. "Oops, sorry." She said in a hushed tone.

Kiriuk directed them to a small clearing where they settled and made camp. He flopped onto the ground next to the fire when the tents were set. "Phew! I'm so tired. All that running, and I was tense the entire time."

"We all were tense. If that guy had spotted us, we could have been thrown in jail or worse," Alistain commented as he sat beside Kiriuk.

"Nah, we could have taken them on," Tsuki said as she clenched her fist.

"Yes, but would that have been very diplomatic of us?" Takagi said sternly as he slapped the back of Tsuki's head and walked by with his bedroll in his other hand. This made Willianna giggle.

"Ow!" Tsuki complained. "Yeah, I guess you're right. I need to think of the bigger picture more often, huh?"

"There you go!" said Alistain, clapping once in victory.

They carried this victory with them as they continued forward.

Chapter Fifteen

No Rest for the Wicked

TSUKI AWOKE AFTER a deep sleep, making a big yawn, "Man, that was a good rest. I didn't even dream of anything. And I didn't wake up in the middle of the night like last time," Tsuki said quietly as she started to get ready for the day.

She looked around the tent for one of her boots and noticed that Alistain was already up and out of the tent. She must have really slept hard for him to get up without waking her. Tsuki sighed as she laced her boots. If only every night was like that.

Tsuki heard people walking outside the tent. The distinct voice of her friend, Willianna, cut through the air. "I can't believe it. We're finally in Heltavin! It seems like forever since we set out on this little adventure," she laughed. Tsuki smiled at her friend's enthusiasm.

It had been about two weeks since they first encountered the Heltavin bandits. That seemed like a while ago to Tsuki, especially because of all that had happened to them since then.

As Tsuki exited the tent, she was greeted by the many smiling faces of her friends. They were already finishing their breakfast, and Takagi was starting to clean up.

Willianna finished her meal and sat facing Tsuki. She smiled when she noticed her friend approaching. Kiriuk was poking the fire and trying to tell a joke. He wasn't very successful, and as he said the punchline, no one laughed but him. Takagi was putting some supplies into the cart. He looked deep in thought.

The others cheered as she walked over. They were mocking her for sleeping so late. She usually was one of the first to get up, along with Takagi.

"There's my sleeping beauty," said Alistain as he patted the spot beside him on the mat they had laid down last night. He had already finished his breakfast of raw meat and fresh blood that was specifically for him. Of course, it was animal blood, not human blood, as that would breach his contract with

Whitiker. Tsuki could see he was writing in his journal but couldn't distinguish the words.

Tsuki sat down next to her lover and laughed. "You should have woken me," she mentioned.

Alistain shrugged, "I tried, but you wouldn't budge. So, I let you sleep."

"Besides, he couldn't stop saying how cute you looked while sleeping," Kiriuk teased as he walked behind Alistain and rubbed the man's shoulders. The wolfman had a grin so wide his fangs were visible.

Alistain shrugged Kiriuk's hands off himself and averted his gaze from Tsuki. He was distinctly blushing.

"Aww, he's shy," Willianna said as she stood up with her plate of finished breakfast. She then laughed as Alistain gave her a look that said, 'Shut up.'

As she was handed a plate of eggs and bacon, Tsuki shook her head, "That man is not shy, I'll tell you that."

"Ooo!" Kiriuk and Willianna said cheekily as they looked at each other and laughed.

Takagi just sighed as he handed Tsuki her morning cup of coffee. Tsuki thanked him as she took a deep sip of the black liquid and hummed appreciatively. As the warm fluid traveled down Tsuki's throat, she felt more awake.

The group cleaned the campsite after Tsuki scarfed down her food and coffee. Today, it was Tsuki's job to take down the tents and extinguish the fire, which was barely going by then. It was mainly smolders and ash but had some flame left. Only after Tsuki finished her chores did she notice everyone else was done. Takagi was even sitting on the cart, waiting for Kiriuk and Alistain to finish saddling their horses and get ready to ride.

"We're going to stop in the next town for supplies. We are low on fresh meat and blood for Alistain, and we need more cooking supplies for the rest of us," Takagi said as he restlessly shifted in the seat on top of the cart.

"Isn't the next town like half a day away?" Willianna whined as she looked at the map while sitting next to Takagi.

Takagi chuckled, "It's on the way we are going. Besides any other direction, we would go off our main course. And..."

"Don't tell me to behave again. I'm tired of hearing those words, Takagi," Kiriuk said with a stomp, startling his horse.

"Well then, don't act like a child all the time," Alistain chided the younger male as he tightened a strap on his saddle.

Kiriuk huffed as he mounted his horse. He was clearly pouting, which would resolve after they were on the road.

It took them most of the day to end up in the next town. It was a bustling place with a marketplace and everything. It was much livelier than all the small villages they had passed through.

The market was easy to see down the main road into town. Many people were there buying, trading, or simply conversing with one another. The town seemed happy enough, with no dreary atmosphere in sight.

As they entered town, they heard two elderly ladies talking. Willianna told Takagi to stop so they could eavesdrop on the conversation.

"Oh dear, Anna. Have you heard about Joelain?" asked one of the old ladies crocheting on a porch beside her friend. She was sitting in a high-backed rocking chair on the porch of a small house. Her gray hair was made up into a ponytail that laid itself on her shoulder.

"Yes!" said the one named Anna. "Another taken by the Swamp of Woes." This elderly woman had gray hair braided and in a top knot, wrapped into a huge ball on her head. She had a big green blanket across her lap with some sewing work, and she sat in a padded chair with very ornate woodwork. She had a very distinct smile with lines around her mischievous eyes.

"We're not from around here," Kiriuk said as he walked his horse up to the women. "So, what's with this swamp you old ladies are talking about?"

Tsuki hopped off Alistain's horse, "Kiriuk! Don’t be rude and nosy!" she hissed quietly as she quickly walked to her friend. Her face was a mix of anger, shock, and embarrassment. She pulled his reins and guided the horse away from the elderly women. "So sorry, my brother doesn't mind his manners. We're sorry for your loss." Tsuki gave Kiriuk a sharp look to let him know she was furious with him.

"Oh, don't worry, dear," Anna said, "We didn't really know the boy. Just sad that anyone would go into that accursed place," she continued, working on her sewing, still not bothering to look up.

"You folks must be adventurers. Most in Heltavin know about the Swamp of Woes," said the other old lady, also not looking up from her crochet.

"Do you mind telling us about this swamp since we are new here? My name's Willianna, by the way," Willianna asked with a smile, hopping down from the cart and walking up to the old ladies.

"Oh, I don't know, Lanna, should we?" Anna laughed.

"Oh, I don't see any harm in it, do you, Anna?" teased Lanna with a chuckle.

"As long as they promise not to go in," Anna replied, looking at Willianna.

"You know we can't promise that," Tsuki said with a shrug.

"We are adventurers, after all," Kiriuk bragged, puffing out his chest.

Right after he said that a young girl ran up to the group and the old ladies. She was running hard and looked like she was crying.

"Lanna! Anna! My older brother went into the Swamp of Woes!" the little girl gasped.

"What? Why?" asked the two old ladies.

"He was dared to by his friend Jaken!" the distressed little girl said, panting.

"Okay, now you have to tell us about the swamp. We have to go find him!" Tsuki said with a decisive tone.

"You'll go after my brother?" the little girl cried.

"Of course, little one," Willianna reassured as she wiped the tears away from the girl's eyes.

"It is a place where the swamp is cursed by an old magic," started Lanna. "The swamp makes you disoriented and uses your fears to distract you."

"You can get lost easily from your fears and die from fright or starvation," said Anna with a frown.

"Woah. An entire swamp that is cursed like that? Amazing!" Kiriuk muttered with excitement in his voice. Alistain punched him in the arm. "Ow!"

"Be considerate, you fool," Alistain whispered. Then he addressed the women, “Do you wonderful ladies mind watching our cart and horses while we go retrieve the boy?" he asked.

Lanna put down her knitting, a little blush on her cheek, "Oh, of course not!"

And with that, the group dismounted and ran off toward the swamp, leaving the cart and horses with the elderly women. They readied their weapons as they left the town, bracing themselves for what might come.

As they kept moving, they ran into puddles of water that had stagnated. Their awful smell almost made the group gag, especially for those with heightened senses. The road turned into a path that was more narrow than before. They had to run in a single file line. Soon, they were at the entrance of the swamp. As the party went through the beginning of the wretched water, the fragrance of the swamp got worse still. The water in the swamp looked blackish, and the fog encapsulated it, making it hard to see. The fog had a sickly green color to it. The trees they could see looked dead and withered and were scattered around.

Tsuki was the first to step into the fog, knowing their objective was important and there was no time to lose. As she entered the fog, it enveloped her so the rest of the group could barely see her. She called back to them, "Stay close. We don't want to lose each other."

"Right!" said her friends.

After a few seconds, the rest of the group entered the fog. They stayed about an arm's length from each other, focusing on the ground to ensure they didn't lose footing due to loose dirt. As they walked, they called for the boy, calling his name into the abyss.

Soon, they heard a cry in the fog. It sounded like a young boy crying for help, but with the swamp's strange sounds, they weren't sure.

"Where are you?" Tsuki yelled as they came to a crossroads.

Unfortunately, because the boy's cry reverberated in the fog, it was impossible to tell which direction he was.

"We have to split up. I'll go with Tsuki and go right while the rest of you go left. We meet back up here in ten minutes, with or without the boy," Takagi said decisively. He knew no one else would make the call in these circumstances, so he made the hard decision.

"Okay, but be safe," Alistain voiced as he reached out to grab Tsuki's hand. He missed as she had started to walk away.

"Okay. Let's go, Takagi," Tsuki stated as she moved down the right path.

Tsuki and Takagi continued to call for the boy but heard no responses. Soon, they started to hear voices other than their own. Tsuki stopped, which made Takagi run into her.

"Sorry," she muttered, "I could have sworn I heard a voice I knew. It must be this fog getting to me."

"I hear the voices, too," Takagi confirmed.

They walked a little further, and Tsuki saw something move in the fog out of the corner of her eye. It looked like a small child, so she took off running. Takagi tried to chase her. After running for a while, Tsuki saw another shadow of a small child running down a side path. Tsuki ran after the shadow, causing her to be separated from Takagi.

The path she was taking wound and intersected several others. Soon, she was lost in the green fog. She slowed to a walk and then stopped, realizing her error.

"Well, crud!" Tsuki cried. "Takagi?" she called as she looked around. Hearing no reply, she knew she was lost.

Tsuki then started hearing the voices again. They were unintelligible whispers before, but now they were actual sentences.

"You've failed your friends."

"You'll never find the boy."

"You should give up."

These voices were all negative statements attacking her self-esteem. Her running off and leaving her friend had already done that. She started to backtrack to find her friend, but the only thing progressing was how aggressive the voices got. And some of the voices started to feel eerily familiar.

"Queen? You? Hah!"

"You will lead them to ruin."

"You will never be a good leader."

Some of those words stung true to her heart. She had always feared failing her country. So much so that she started to tear up. Tsuki wiped the tears away and kept moving, even though she had no idea where she was going. Soon, she came to a dead end.

"Great. What am I supposed to do now?" Tsuki asked herself into the fog. She raised her arms as if expecting an answer. When no answer came, she let her arms drop to her side.

Then, out of nowhere, there were two shadows on either side of her. They looked like grown people and were coming closer. Soon, they started to speak.

"You think you can get away from me?" said one, the voice burning into Tsuki's ears. She knew that voice. The voice was sickeningly high but distinctly a man's voice.

"You are nothing!" snarled the other shadow. That voice, too, was familiar. The voice sounded like someone with arrogance.

"Who are you? Stop this farce!" Tsuki commanded.

"You? Command me? A king?" yelled one shadow. It soon was close to her. Tsuki could see who it was. It was Lentus.

"You can't get rid of me. I'm with you always," taunted the other shadow. She knew who it was even before she turned to look. Dr. Gruten stood before her.

"No! You both aren't real!" Tsuki yelled as she took a step backward. She then felt like she was on a tiny island with nowhere to go. The fright she felt from looking at the two figures before her sent an icy chill to her heart.

"You've failed! We are here forever!" yelled Lentus.

"I will cut you open!" Gruten cried.

The shadows advanced on Tsuki's position. Tsuki started to swing her clawed hands at them. But the claws went through the shadows whenever she thought she would connect.

"Why. Won't. You. Die!" Tsuki yelled, punctuating each word with a swing of her claws. She was crying, scared, confused. She didn't know what to do.

"We are eternal," screeched Gruten.

"We will always be with you," Lentus bellowed.

Soon, the shadows were on top of her. She shrunk down into a ball and cried. She covered her head with her hands and just sobbed. "Stop it! Stop it!" she screamed.

Suddenly, something stirred inside Tsuki. A power she hadn’t used in decades. All she knew was that she must scream. It was a primal sound; when she did so, intense heat flowed through her. Her back hurt, and she saw a bright light through her closed eyes.

The pain in her back was her wings bursting forth. The pain from the wings exiting her body was sharp and overwhelming. They were the wings she had first used while escaping the one who killed her parents and the time when her rage got the best of her.

The white light pierced through the mystic fog of the swamp and created a crater around Tsuki. Her wings began cocooning her body.

Then, the voices finally stopped. Tsuki lay in the crater, unconscious.

Chapter Sixteen
The Swamp of Woes

AS TSUKI RAISED her head from the ground, she noticed that most of the fog had cleared. Rocks were falling all around her, and she saw her friends in the distance trying to dodge them. The crater that Tsuki had made was filled with blackish-green water.

"Tsuki!" Alistain cried. He used his vampiric-enhanced jump to get to her. He quickly and expertly picked her up bridal style and jumped back to Willianna and Kiriuk. "My love... was... was that you?"

"Why are your wings out?" asked Willianna.

"I remember having them when I fought that werewolf with Alistain a while back. And when I ran away from Gruten, something similar happened." Tsuki whispered.

Takagi had transformed himself into a hawk and flew over to the others. As he flew, he called, "My lady Tsuki, are you alright?" When Takagi came in for a landing, he shapeshifted into his human form.

"I thought you, of all people, would take care of her." Alistain stabbed as he glared at Takagi.

"She's the one who ran off without me! How was I supposed to know?" Takagi countered with a glare of his own. He then looked at Tsuki with a softened gaze. "How are you feeling?"

"I'm fine. Just weak." Tsuki remarked quietly.

"Your power must have drained you since you obviously don't have a handle on it yet," said a female voice behind the group.

The group immediately turned around to find an elderly woman with spiral goat horns and a single straight horn protruding from her forehead. On top of her head was a pair of goggles that looked to be made out of green glass. She was wearing a ratty brown robe with a hood on the back. Her feet shuffled forward as she walked toward the group. Her bright pink eyes pierced Tsuki's.

"Who are you?" Tsuki asked, her voice wavering from exhaustion.

"That is of no importance," waved the old hag. "First, let's get your strength up, hm, Moon Warrior?" She then pointed past the group, who turned around only to see an old hut at the edge of the crater Tsuki made.

They slowly made their way to the hut in silence. None of them knew what to ask this hag who came out of nowhere.

Soon, the hag entered the hut and directed Alistain to lay the weakened Tsuki on the bed in the corner. Everyone else filed into the small structure after the hag invited them in. The hag shuffled over to a stovetop and put a kettle on top of it. She then walked over to a cabinet next to the stove and grabbed a cup and a handful of what seemed to be spices.

Everyone was quiet, watching what she was doing. She whispered into the furnace underneath the stovetop, which suddenly caught fire. She straightened herself and nodded in triumph.

"Well, don't just stare at the back of my head. Talk! Converse! Ask me questions!" commanded the hag as she suddenly turned around, making everyone jump.

"Well, umm... how do you know about Tsuki's powers?" Takagi asked, shifting uncomfortably where he stood.

"I know those wings. Those wings were given to her long before she was born by the Moon Goddess. Nothing in this world can grow wings like that," the hag answered. "Next!"

There was a beat of silence before Willianna spoke. "So, what happened to her? What was that light?"

"She used her full power. So now she's drained of energy. She should avoid doing that as it can severely harm her, and she will not heal as quickly as normal," the hag said as the kettle whistled. The hag grabbed the hot kettle and poured a liquid that didn't seem to be water into the cup with the spices. She then picked up the cup and walked it over to Tsuki. "Let it steep and cool down before you drink it, dear." The hag said gently as she handed Tsuki the cup of liquid.

"Thank you." Tsuki responded weakly. Her hands shook slightly as she raised them to grab the cup.

"Why did you call her Moon Warrior?" Kiriuk asked, his ears twitching as he waited for the answer.

"Yeah. What is that?" queried Takagi.

"Well, that's what she is. She's been chosen by the Moon Goddess to be a great leader. You were all told the stories of us being created from the moon as little l'uns, right? The legend goes, 'You are made from stardust and light from the moon.' Anyway, basically, she is a median between the light and the dark. So, of course, she has the powers of a god and a demon mixed deep inside her. But this power is limited by her flesh body. And as I can see from her ears and tail, she must be a werewolf too," the hag explained as she walked over to a chair and sat.

"So you're saying a legend that I, the court wizard, have never heard of is true? You must be on something." Takagi said as he stepped forward in an exasperated tone.

The hag laughed, "Me being on something is neither here nor there. What is important is that she masters her powers before this happens again. You were all lucky that you were far enough away.

Otherwise, you would have been seriously injured. And we don't want that now, do we, dear?"

"So what do I need to do?" Tsuki asked as she sipped the beverage she was told was tea. She wasn't sure if that was true. It tasted earthy, like tea set out for too long, with a hint of lemon.

"You need to find that feeling you had before. Try it now while you're still weak enough; it won't hurt anyone if you use it." the hag said as she pointed to Tsuki's chest.

"Okay..." Tsuki vocalized hesitantly.

She handed Alistain her cup and sat up. He was clinging to her like the pages of a book. She took a deep breath and closed her eyes. She replayed the scene of being in the fog over in her mind. She then tried to focus on the moment of warmth she felt while she was scared. Soon, that was all she felt, and everything else fell away.

To the others, Tsuki was focused and concentrating on something. After a while of her sitting still, a light in the shape of an orb emerged from her chest and hovered above her hands resting on her legs. It was a strange and tense sight as Tsuki's friends and the hag watched with bated breath.

"Good," the old hag said, "Now try opening your eyes."

As Tsuki complied, she opened her eyes, staring at the white orb floating before her. "What is that?" Tsuki asked.

"Why, my dear. That's your true power." the old hag cheered as she clapped her hands excitedly. "You pick up quickly, don't cha."

Tsuki lifted one of her hands and tentatively poked the orb. It felt warm, just like her body when she accidentally used her power. Her finger passed right into it and tingled briefly until she pulled it out. She was no longer thinking or focusing on the feeling of her body, and she was concentrating on the orb. She marveled at how it looked and felt. As she was about to laugh, the orb shrunk and exploded into sprinkles of light that drifted downward.

"Aw..." said Tsuki as she watched the flickering lights fall.

"You must have stopped focusing on it, my girl. That's why it went away. You need to train on harnessing that feeling and moving it to other parts of your body," the hag mentioned as she got up from her seat. She shuffled over to the bed, snatched the cup from Alistain's hands, and handed it to Tsuki. "But for now, rest."

Tsuki took another sip. She was already feeling better. As she sipped on the liquid, she remembered something and nearly choked.

"Oh, crap! The boy!" Tsuki fell into a coughing fit at how forcefully she yelled.

"Language, my lady," Takagi said, even though he was concerned about her choking.

Alistain was patting her on the back, trying to get the coughing to stop.

"Oh, shut up!" Tsuki remarked through her coughs. "We have to go find him!" Tsuki jumped up from the bed as she handed Alistain the cup again. She ran to the door of the small cottage and opened it. What she saw made her heart drop. The fog was back.

"Great... now we'll never find him or get back to town," Willianna sighed.

There was a giant, annoyed sigh from the rest of the group.

"Wait. How do you get back to town through this fog?" Alistain asked the hag.

"Well. I use these, of course." The hag smiled as she reached for the goggles on her head. "They are made from volcanic glass and hold special properties that let me see through the fog."

"Can we have them?" Kiriuk asked excitedly.

"No!" said the hag sternly.

"Oh..." Kiriuk replied in defeat. His shoulders slumped, and his head hung low.

"But, you can have those over there," the hag mentioned with a laugh. She pointed to a glass case filled with odd trinkets of all sorts. One of those trinkets was a second pair of green goggles.

"Are you serious?" Tsuki asked. "You'd give us those?"

The hag nodded. "Seeing how you are the Moon Warrior, how could I not?" She walked over to the case and opened it. The hag grabbed the goggles and handed them to Tsuki, who closed her hand over them. "See this as a loan for when you bring peace to the world." The hag winked at Tsuki.

"O...kay." Tsuki said as the hag let go. Tsuki put on the goggles and looked back out into the fog. She could see much further than before. She could actually see the path and some of the crater.

"Alright, everyone! Hold hands, and I'll try and find the boy as we go." Tsuki said with a nod.

"Right!" said the rest of the group as they interlocked their hands.

As Tsuki walked forward, she focused on the path to the crater's right. While walking, she told the others about precarious places on the path. The others were grateful. While Tsuki focused on walking and directing, the rest of the group decided to call out for the boy.

After a while of careful movement, Kiriuk's ears perked up. "Wait, I hear something!" he shouted. This made everyone stop. "I hear crying. That direction." He let go of Willianna's hand and pointed off into the distance. He quickly grabbed Willianna's hand again to ensure he wasn't lost.

"There's a path headed that way. I'll follow it." Tsuki announced as she started walking to the path that led in the direction that Kiriuk pointed.

On her way, Tsuki noticed the dark waters turning into a black, goo-like substance. She dismissed it and didn't mention it as she was distracted looking for the boy.

Soon, she also started to hear crying. Tsuki resisted the urge to run to the boy and leave her friends behind; she knew better now. Her wings flapped silently, and her ears twitched at the thought of how mad Alistain and Takagi would be if she did that.

Tsuki started to walk faster, which made the hand-holding harder for everyone. After walking hurriedly in the fog, the boy crying sounded like he was right next to them. Tsuki stopped and looked around her.

She halted so quickly that she made all the others run into each other and nearly fall down into the black goop. As she looked around, Tsuki noticed movement out of the corner of her eye. It was the boy! She then let go of Alistain's hand and knelt down to get a better look at the boy's situation. He had fallen into the black substance and was slowly sinking. He was now up to his torso in goo.

"Hey, kid!" Tsuki yelled.

The boy stopped rubbing his eyes and crying and looked up at her. "Who are you? Why are you here?"

"Your sister sent us to look for you. Let's get you out of there, huh?" Tsuki said with a smile as she reached out and grabbed the boy's arm. She then tried to pull him out with no success.

"If only we had better leverage!" said Takagi.

"Leverage? I have an idea!" Tsuki said as she stood up. "Kid, I'm going to need you to raise your arms as high as you can."

The boy did as he was told. Tsuki then took a few steps back and ran at the boy as she started to flap her wings. Once she got to the pathway's edge, she jumped and took off flying while reaching for the boy's arms. She grabbed them and started to flap to try and get him out of the goop, but the bog was dense and held on tight. Tsuki flapped as hard as she could. The boy slowly came free. Once he was free, Tsuki instinctively flew them back to the group, dropping him gently as she made another round and landed.

"Woah. How'd I do that?" Tsuki asked as she flapped her wings once more.

Takagi stepped forward and ran a gentle hand over Tsuki's feathers. "It's instinct. Just like when I turn into a hawk. I can do maneuvers I would have never thought of. Just go with the flow, Tsuki."

Alistain cleared his throat as he glared at Takagi.

Takagi retracted his hand quickly and said, "I mean, my lady."

Tsuki helped the boy to stand. "Why don't you walk with us, and we'll find our way back to the town, okay?"

"Okay." sniffed the boy.

Tsuki took one of his hands, and Alistain took the other. The rest of the party took the hint that they were about to move again and grabbed hands.

It took them about half an hour to finally escape the swamp. The occasional curse or hateful word was thrown into the abyss at the shadows that tried to come for the individuals in the group. Thankfully, they had each other to calm them down when things got intense. Once they reached the edge of the fog and, subsequently, the swamp's edge, everyone heaved a huge sigh of relief.

They then returned to the town, boy in tow, who was now on Kiriuk's shoulders. When they were in sight of the two old ladies who were watching the cart, they saw the little girl. She was obviously crying as she paced back and forth. Once she saw the group come into view, she ran towards them, crying even more.

"Big brother! You're alive!" she said.

Kiriuk let down the boy, who ran to his sister.

"I'm sorry. I should have never let them talk me into going. Let's go tell mom I'm ok."

The group approached the cart and horses as the two children ran off. Takagi lifted the tarp to make sure nothing had been stolen.

"No one messed with your things, young adventurers." said Lanna.

"Though I am surprised you came back at all," said Anna.

Before anyone could open their mouths to tell the elderly women what had happened in the swamp, Kiriuk said, "Well, that's just how good we are."

This made the old ladies laugh.

That night, they stayed in the inn of the town. Comfy beds and a meal other than plain bread and meat hit the spot. The group was exhausted and fell asleep easily, another trial behind them.

Chapter Seventeen

Sharing is Caring

WHEN TSUKI AWOKE, she wasn't in her tent or in a room at an inn. She was lying on her stomach on a slab of dark marble. Around her was black smoke and water on the ground. She heard footsteps in the distance and called, "Who's there?" but got no reply. She wrote it off as water dripping in the distance.

Tsuki got up and noticed the marble slab she was on was actually floating on the water. It was unsteady, but she took her time noticing how it moved and stood fully upright soon enough. The water became jet black with more observation, but Tsuki could see into it.

After looking around for a while and trying to decipher her surroundings, Tsuki noticed something in the smoke. Looking down at the water, she noticed something circling the marble platform. She had an eerie feeling that something would happen, which wasn't good.

Then, suddenly, Tsuki heard a strong gust of wind coming and braced for it. It rocked the marble slab back and forth in the water and made her change her footing. Tsuki looked into the wind to see what was causing it and found the smoke had cleared and that a single person was walking toward her on top of the water.

As the person got closer, Tsuki noticed that it was Lentus in his usual purple cloak and crown.

"You again?" Tsuki readied her stance to fight. "Why can't you and Gruten just leave me alone?"

When she said Dr. Gruten's name, the marble slab started to rock even more. This made Tsuki look down and see the creepy smiling face of the doctor coming out of the water, the rest of his body submerged in the blackness.

When Tsuki saw who was rocking her footing, she instinctively jumped back to get away. She was on the water's surface when she landed and could stand like Lentus. She was shocked at this new development, saying, "What is this place?"

"We've been here numerous times, little girl," Lentus said as he kept walking, closing the gap between him and Tsuki.

"It should be like home to you now," smiled Dr. Gruten. He was using the marble slab Tsuki had been on to pull himself out of the water till he could stand.

Tsuki readied her stance again for a fight. This was one of the few dreams where she could actually move her legs, so she would take advantage of it. She took a deep, calming breath to ready herself for a fight with her worst enemies.

Lentus stopped walking as he got next to the dripping-wet Gruten. Lentus then got in a fighting stance as well and readied his magic. Gruten just laughed maniacally.

"No! Shut up!" Tsuki yelled as she charged the two men.

Gruten jumped out of the way, and Lentus shot a spell of purple magic at Tsuki, which she easily dodged. Tsuki then jumped at Lentus and tried to kick at his head. Unfortunately, he dodged it as well, sending Tsuki flying towards Gruten, who, by that time, had pulled out a scalpel and was charging at Tsuki when she landed. Tsuki blocked the scalpel and gave Gruten a gut punch, which knocked him off his feet.

Sadly, Tsuki didn't have much time to think as Lentus fired a purple fireball in her direction. She did a backflip and barely missed the fireball by half an inch.

When she landed, she started to panic. She did not know if she could beat Lentus alone while dealing with Gruten. Lentus was an expert wizard, and it would be difficult. If only she had a grasp on her Moon Warrior powers.

"That's it!" Tsuki exclaimed. All she had to do was use her inner strength, and they would be toast. And to do it, she just needed to focus on the feeling and dodge their attacks. She would do this on the fly, but it was the only way to defeat them.

Tsuki focused on finding the warm feeling again as Lentus charged another bigger fireball. Gruten was still getting up from the gut punch that Tsuki had delivered. She was under pressure to find the feeling, but somehow, a little flame of warmth was already in her heart; she just had to grasp it. Once she did, she focused on spreading it throughout her body.

She didn't have much time as Lentus had thrown his fireball at her. Thankfully, she was aware of her surroundings, jumped to the side, and rolled out of the way just in time. Standing up, Tsuki refocused on the warmth and got it to her left arm. As she did that, a small ball of white light appeared in her left hand, and it was growing. She didn't have to spread it to all of her body, just the part she was using, just like the hag said.

Suddenly, from behind, Gruten yelled as he charged Tsuki, scalpel clasped in his hands, ready to strike. As he got closer, Tsuki focused on growing the ball of light. Soon, it was the size of a small throwing ball that kids played with. She turned and dodged Gruten's attack and used the ball of light to strike at his back. This sent him flying across the expansive room, but Tsuki wasn't sure how big it was when she released it.

After flying a second or two, Gruten came into contact with an invisible wall, making a hard thud. He then fell to the ground, dazed. Now, all Tsuki had to worry about was making another ball of light to finish Lentus. However, she didn't have time to create another ball as Lentus charged with a lightning bolt in his hand.

"You are nothing!" Lentus yelled as he ran.

"Ya wanna bet?" Tsuki said as she jumped over her attacker and rolled to her feet. She was biding her time until she had another ball formed. She felt the warmth returning to her left arm and saw it forming. She knew it wouldn't be long until she could strike.

As she turned around, she sidestepped and miraculously dodged a lightning bolt flying at her head.

After dodging a few more lightning bolts from Lentus, Tsuki looked down and saw that her ball of light was bigger than before. So, she charged Lentus at full speed with her hand behind her, ready to throw it. Lentus had already established a magical barrier by the time she was in range. That didn't stop Tsuki from trying to plow through it with her strike. The ball of light warped as she pressed it against the magical wall, and soon, the wall shattered, and the ball returned to its original shape. It connected with Lentus' chest and kept going, blowing out the back of the man's body. But there were no guts or blood. Just darkness.

Tsuki stopped herself from falling with the body of her foe. She was victorious and used her newfound power to do it. Sure, she needed to figure out how to use it better, so she didn't kill someone, but it was an improvement.

As she started to cheer, Tsuki saw a bright light above her. A familiar, warm voice said, "It's time to get up." It was a woman's voice, soft and soothing. The light got brighter and brighter. Tsuki felt herself being lifted like she was weightless. Soon, the light engulfed her, and she awoke.

She awoke in the bed of the inn they stayed at. She looked around and found Alistain lying on his side facing her, head in his hand.

"Well, well, look who's up. You were tossing and turning there for a bit. Another nightmare?" Alistain said as he sat up and took Tsuki's hand, kissing her knuckles.

Tsuki sat up as well and looked back behind her. Her wings were gone. That was okay with her because they made her stick out in the crowd last night. She then told Alistain what happened in her dream with every detail.

"I won!" Tsuki said excitedly, bouncing into Alistain's arms.

"That's amazing!" Alistain smiled as he gave her an excited kiss on the lips. "I'm so proud that you faced your fears and won! This deserves something special." He said as he leaned in close and gave Tsuki a deeper kiss.

She knew what he meant with his devious smile.

Tsuki then wrapped her arms around Alistain's neck and kissed him hard. "Oh?" She teased.

As they kissed, they didn't even hear the knock at the door. Willianna opened the door to find the two lovers intertwined with each other.

"My, my. You two start early," Willianna said as she leaned against the doorway. This snapped the two lovers out of their haze of bliss and brought them back to reality.

Tsuki quickly separated herself from Alistain as she turned bright red. "Wha-what are you doing here!?" Tsuki asked.

"Well... I was sent up here to get you guys for breakfast. We've been waiting for a good while for you to come down," Willianna explained as she laughed at Tsuki's reaction.

"We'll be down in a minute." said Alistain as he got up from the bed.

"All right, you two. Don't keep us waiting too long." Willianna said with a wink to Tsuki, who was hiding behind the bedsheets in embarrassment.

Alistain chuckled, walked around to Tsuki's side of the bed, and kissed her deeply, holding the back of her head to keep her in place. After a while of kissing, Alistain broke away.

"Let's get up, hm?" he said as he turned away from Tsuki. He looked over his shoulder at her and gave her a wink that sent her blushing again, making her hide behind the covers.

As they dressed, Alistain kept giving Tsuki soft kisses on her cheeks and lips. It took them twice as long to get dressed as it normally would. Mostly because Tsuki kept getting flustered.

When they finally came down from their room, their friends cheered. Takagi waved over the innkeeper's wife and asked for breakfast for them. She nodded and walked away to get the food ready.

"Took you long enough," Kiriuk laughed.

"I told you they were preoccupied," Willianna said, being coy.

"Preoccupied with what?" Kiriuk asked, oblivious to what she really meant.

"Forget it. They are here now, and that's what matters." Takagi said, clapping to get the two troublemakers' attention.

As Tsuki and Alistain sat, albeit a little blushed from what Willianna said, the innkeeper's wife came back with a plate of fried eggs and ham. She was followed by her young daughter carrying a plate of toast.

"Thank you." Kiriuk said as he watched the young girl place the plate before him. She giggled at him and ran away, blushing, much to Kiriuk's confusion.

"Anyway," Kiriuk stated as he shook his head clear of his confusion. "I had a horrible nightmare of what I saw in the swamp. Did anyone else?"

"I did. But nightmares are normal for me. What was yours about?" asked Tsuki as she shoved some eggs onto her plate. "I've told you about what I saw in the fog, so it's your turn."

"Yeah, I guess," Willianna sassed at Tsuki, who stuck her tongue out in response.

"Now, ladies..." Alistain chuckled at the two friends. "Tsuki has a point. Why don't we all share?"

"Alright! Since I brought the topic up, I'll go first," Kiriuk said as he shoved a piece of toast into his mouth, much to Takagi's dismay.

Everyone settled in and started eating. Kiriuk started to tell what he saw in the fog the day before.

"In the fog, all I could hear was all of you crying out in pain and yelling for my help. I couldn't run to help because then I would get lost." Kiriuk said as he ate. "And as we walked, trying to find the boy, I saw dead bodies. The bodies looked like all of you. It scared me really bad." He shivered as he said the last sentence. It obviously disturbed him deeply as he was recounting the events. The group wasn’t used to seeing him like this. There was a long pause of silence, and then he looked up as cheerful as ever and asked, "What about you, Willianna?"

Kiriuk had asked right when Willianna had taken a bite of her eggs. She nearly choked when she heard her name. "Umm..." she said as she chewed, covering her mouth so she did not show her food. "Well, all I heard and saw was my mom. We had plans to bring her to Urufu for a few months since my brother was moving away from the village to marry some harlot. And the thought of her dying along the way..." Willianna's face grew somber. "Well, that better not happen," she declared as she moved her eggs around the plate.

"I heard Whitiker yelling at me," Alistain said as he watched his friends eat. "He said I broke my promises, drank from someone, and ran away from my duties. Which is not true. But what I saw in the fog dropped my heart. I saw him dragging me away from you, my love," he said to Tsuki. "I could not resist him as I am bound by a blood oath. And the thought of never seeing you again would break me," Alistain grasped and held tightly to Tsuki's hand.

"That won't happen, okay?" Tsuki said to try to quiet Alistain's fears.

Takagi sighed and took a sip of his coffee. When he put it down, he said, "I saw something deeply personal, and I'd rather not talk about it."

"Oh, come on," said Kiriuk.

"We all shared, so you have to as well," Willianna countered.

After a moment of thinking, Takagi finally gave in, "Alright." He said, "But I don't want anyone saying anything about it once I'm done."

Everyone nodded their heads in agreement. Kiriuk even gave him a thumbs up.

Takagi took a deep breath and started, "It was losing Tsuki again. After spending years trying to find her and then losing her in the fog... I saw you dying or being dragged away, crying out for me to save you.

But I was powerless to do so. I was useless. I never want to see that again, to feel that again." He said with tears in his eyes. Staring into Tsuki's silver and blue ones.

There was a very long pause of silence. No one dared be the first to speak. They didn't know what to say. But it was Tsuki who broke the silence.

"Thank you for sharing Takagi," Tsuki said. It was quiet, yet because of the silence, it sounded louder than it really was and made Takagi jump.

"You are welcome, my lady," Takagi bowed slightly as he returned to his meal.

"Why are you suddenly calling me 'my lady' again? You had been calling me by my name before. Why the sudden change?" Tsuki asked with a tilt of her head. She had thought it was odd for some time but could never catch him doing it.

"I don't know what you are talking about," Takagi refuted as he took another sip of coffee.

"I'm not the only one who's noticed it, right?" Tsuki asked as she looked around the table.

"I guess. But it's not like it's a big deal or anything," Willianna shrugged.

"She's right, sis. I would just let it go," Kiriuk said through a mouthful of egg.

Takagi looked at Alistain and saw his blood-red eyes staring at him. It was all he could take not to out their conversation right then and there. "I'm doing it because it's my duty to you. And that's that. So, if you'll please excuse me, I'll start getting the horses ready," Takagi said, obviously upset by how he suddenly stood up and stormed off.

And with that, the rest of the group shoveled their food into their mouths and went after Takagi to help prepare for the morning. They, of course, paid the innkeeper and thanked his wife for the meal. Then, soon after, they were on the road to the Heltavin capital.

Chapter Eighteen

The Capital

TSUKI RUNS THROUGH an unfamiliar forest. Why? She didn't know. All she knew was she had to get away and fast. Suddenly, a lightning bolt flew by her head as she ran.

"Oh yeah," she muttered.

As she jumped over a log, a giant sword swung out of the shadows and cut the log in half, barely missing Tsuki. This scared her and made her stumble.

A laugh out of the darkness behind her sent chills down her spine. It wasn't a deep laugh like Lentus's nor high-pitched like the doctor's. She had no idea who was chasing her, so she looked back behind her. She saw a person with short hair, glowing pink eyes, and a wide knowing smile.

As she looked back, she tripped over the root of a tree. Rolling and tumbling, Tsuki soon came to a stop. Her hair was everywhere and had a few scuffs, but otherwise, she was okay. Tsuki then looked back at the darkness behind her. The figure in it was upon her quickly.

The now obviously male figure raised his hands with a lightning bolt in one and the giant sword in the other and said, "I am the emperor. No one will defeat me!" After he was done talking, he swung his sword down at Tsuki.

That's when she woke up. She bolted straight up in her bedroll in the tent she was in. She looked around and found Alistain sleeping soundly beside her, facing away. Tsuki sighed and laid back down, wrapping an arm around Alistain and pulling him close. He mumbled something and smiled as he fell back asleep. Tsuki soon followed.

That morning, Tsuki got ready as usual. As she stepped out of the tent, her eyes locked with Takagi's. She quickly looked away and walked over to Willianna, who was already eating. As she sat, Takagi handed Tsuki a plate without looking at her.

To say things had been a little awkward within the group since the talk at the inn would be an understatement. Takagi gave short orders about housekeeping things but otherwise stayed quiet and stern. He was usually prattling on about what they had to do for that day and how far they were to their destination. But today, that was Alistain's job.

As Alistain sat beside Tsuki, he said, "Today, we should reach the capital. Right, Takagi?"

Takagi didn't say anything; he just kept cooking.

Alistain waited for the response, but it never came. "Well... we should make it there by mid-afternoon if I read the map correctly last night."

"Great!" Kiriuk cheered as he came out of his tent. "Maybe now we'll get some decent breakfast," he laughed as he poked Takagi in the side like it was a joke. When that didn't work, Kiriuk frowned. "Oh, come on, you know I love your cooking!" Kiriuk then wrapped an arm around Takagi's shoulders. "Stop being upset and be like you used to!"

"No. And get off of me." Takagi muttered as he shrugged Kiriuk's arm off. He threw the rest of the food onto a plate, handed it to the wolf, and strode off to set up the cart.

"It's no use," shrugged Willianna as she stood up. "You'll never get him to break. He just has to wallow in his sadness for a while, and then he'll be right as rain. Hurry up and eat so I can do the dishes."

"Yeah, but I worry about him. He's my brother, and I just want him to be like he was," Kiriuk said in protest.

"Yes, but you can't always get what you want. He shared some deeply personal stuff the other day," Tsuki mentioned as she pushed her food around on her plate.

"She's right. He just needs time, Kiriuk." Alistain sighed as he got up from his seat as well. He felt responsible for Takagi's response to Tsuki questioning him about his behavior. If only he had kept his mouth shut, things would be better now. Tsuki might even be enjoying herself instead of worrying about her friends. He shook his head to clear his thoughts and said, "I should take down tents, huh?"

"Right, we'd better get to work!" Kiriuk smiled as he stuffed his face with his plate full of food.

Once they finally got to the capital, they saw bustling streets full of merchants calling out products and people murmuring, trying to get deals and lower prices, no doubt. As they entered the town,

Tsuki noticed that the bricks they had built with were darker than those of Urufu's. And the buildings were two or three stories taller than most buildings in Urufu. But Tsuki guessed that was because they had more people in those buildings or this castle town was smaller than hers. Most of the windows in the buildings were made of colorful stained glass, and extravagant arches everywhere. There were spires everywhere and fierce-looking statues and gargoyles at every turn.

While the streets were busy, the group had enough room to make slow headway, giving them opportunities to look around. One such opportunity came to Kiriuk as they went down the main street.

"Fox here! Live fox! Great for meat and fur!" said a merchant.

This drew Kiriuk's attention, and the young wolfman soon came eye to eye with a brown fox. It whimpered and yelped as the merchant hit the cage he was in.

That's when Kiriuk turned around and looked at Tsuki, riding in front of Alistain on their horse.

"Sis! I need that fox," Kiriuk told her sternly, which was rare for him. He usually was cheery and upbeat.

"What? What fox? Why?" Tsuki asked, puzzled.

Kiriuk pointed as they got closer to the merchant. "That one. He'll likely be killed. And I can't bear the thought that I didn't do something to help him."

"And what are you going to do with him? If you just let him go, he'll probably be trampled by the crowd or be captured again," Tsuki said, shaking her head. It's not like she didn't want to help the fox; it's just that she knew what it was like to run away and be caught again in a whole new mess.

"Yes, but I'll regret it forever if we don't try. Please, Tsuki. I need to save him," Kiriuk pleaded. He was adamant that he needed to save this fox, and it was evident how serious his face was.

"Alright. Go get him," Tsuki said with a sigh. She shook her head but knew that when Kiriuk had his heart set on something, he would do it no matter what. Might as well give his stupidity your blessing than berate him later to no avail.

"Yes! I'll take him!" yelled Kiriuk as he hopped off his horse.

"Wonderful. And that will be five silver," smiled the merchant, holding out his hand greedily.

Kiriuk dug into his pouch at his side and pulled out a few coins. He handed the merchant five silver and returned the rest to his pouch, saying, "Keep the trap. I won't be needing it."

"What are you going to do with him?" The merchant asked, puzzled.

"Nothing you would do, you monster," Kiriuk commented in a low, growly voice as he returned to his horse. As he climbed back into his saddle, he smiled at the fox he held.

"Easy, buddy, you're safe with me." Kiriuk smiled softly.

The fox chirped at Kiriuk and nuzzled into his chest. This made Kiriuk laugh. But as they came to a less dense part of the street, Kiriuk let the fox down.

"There you go, friend. Be safe, okay?" Kiriuk said softly as he waved goodbye, looking back to steering his horse.

"Feel better, little bro?" Tsuki asked with a small smile.

"Ye-..." Kiriuk started to say but cut himself short as he felt something pulling at his tail. He looked down to see what had snagged his tail. It was the brown fox he had just saved. Before Kiriuk could say anything, the fox jumped into his lap and barked.

Kiriuk was puzzled. "Wha?" he questioned as the fox continued to nuzzle into him.

"Looks like you've made a new friend," Willianna chirped in, trying to stifle her giggles.

"Well, I guess so!" Kiriuk mentioned happily.

"What are you going to name him?" Tsuki asked.

Kiriuk thought for a moment as they rode. "Foxy Brown. Because he's brown and a fox!"

Tsuki slapped her forehead in disbelief at how simple Kiriuk could be sometimes.

Kiriuk played with Foxy Brown as they got closer and closer to the castle. It was a dark, dark brick with many buttresses that stood out as extravagant.

Tsuki noticed the increase of guards and fewer commoners as they went further. She thought this was strange since they were on the main street.

Suddenly, as Tsuki was looking at a group of passing guards, another stagnant group threw a rock at her, hitting her in the back of her head.

"Stupid werewolves. Always trying to encroach on our land," said one guard, supposedly the one who threw the rock.

They had seen her tail and ears, not that she or Kiriuk were trying to hide them.

"Yeah! Go back to the forest where you belong, cretin," yelled another guard.

Alistain looked at the rock that had fallen in his lap. It had hints of blood on it. He looked up at Tsuki, who was holding the back of her head and trying to stifle tears.

"Aww, look, the little puppy is crying," cried the first guard. This made the rest of the guards laugh.

"Hey! You. Apologize to her. You drew blood, and that is unforgivable. Just because she's a minority to you humans and us vampires doesn't give you the right," Alistain yelled as he bared his fangs, holding tightly to Tsuki.

"Hey, what's all the ruckus about over here?" said the leader of another group of guards as they walked up.

By now, Takagi had stopped their procession and was turned around in his seat, watching all this happen. Willianna was turned around as well. Kiriuk had reached for his spear on his back, ready for a fight.

"You can't talk to us that way. We're the royal guard," yelled the first guard. He had now drawn his sword and stepped forward. "Get him and teach him a lesson."

Two of the guards ran up to Alistain before he could react. They pulled him off his horse and Tsuki with him because he held on to her. Both hit the ground hard and were dazed for a moment. The two guards then pulled Alistain from Tsuki and started to kick him.

"Stop that!" Tsuki yelled as she stood up and rushed to her lover's side.

By then, Kiriuk had gotten off his horse and took a defensive stance against a few guards. Willianna and Takagi stood on the cart, ready to jump down.

"Detain them!" yelled the first guard. "Get their weapons!"

The guards were suddenly upon Tsuki and the others, pulling at them and yanking them. It happened so fast that Tsuki barely had time to think before they had her bound with her hands behind her back. The rest of her friends were also bound and were being held prisoner. Foxy Brown was nowhere to be seen.

"What's going on here?" asked an important-looking man on a horse as he approached the scene. He looked to be a noble.

"This group was harassing and attacking us," lied the third guard.

"That's not what happened," yelled Willianna, who was bleeding from a scuffed knee, showing she didn't go down without a fight.

"Yeah, they attacked us first," Tsuki said to back up her friend. But once the words left her mouth, she was backhanded by a gauntlet hand.

"Silence, werewolf. You should know your kind isn't welcome here anymore. Not after the emperor decreed that you were less than us humans," commanded the noble.

"What?" Kiriuk mumbled.

"Take them to the throne room. The emperor will decide their fate. Besides, I'm too busy to do such a deplorable thing myself. Don't forget to search the cart for valuables that can be given to the emperor." The noble said as he rode away.

The guards who weren't restraining the group searched the cart. What they found was less than pleasing to Tsuki and her friends.

"Hey, look, I found a map that shows their route. It says they came from the Urufian capital," cried one guard.

"Then we must take them to the emperor for judgment right away, no matter what," affirmed another guard.

They were thrown into the back of the cart and taken by the guards to the castle. Once they entered the gate, there was no turning back. Tsuki swallowed hard as she looked around. They were surrounded by guards.

The group stayed quiet, only sharing glances as they were taken to the center of the capital, the castle that stood tall.

"My emperor Klage," announced one of the guards as they drug Tsuki and her group into the throne room.

The man Tsuki assumed was the emperor was haphazardly sitting on the throne. His long limbs were strewn everywhere on the chair, even with his foot on the edge of the seat. He was pale with dark, black circles under his pink eyes. He had medium-length dark hair that came to his shoulders and a short and kept beard. He wore all black except for a bright red pendant around his neck.

"What now?" the man sitting in the giant chair asked in a monotone voice.

The guards knelt and made Tsuki and her friends kneel as well.

"We have brought these troublemakers to be judged before you," said the kneeling guard.

A man dressed in green with blue pants and a purple bowtie walked forward. He had purple eyes and short, curly gray hair. He looked so small and frail that a strong wind would break him. "Why have you bothered our great emperor with such trivial matters?" the mystery man asked authoritatively.

"Well, my lord, we have evidence that leads us to believe these hooligans are from the capital of Urufu. Maybe a small scouting party," explained the kneeling guard, obviously afraid of the mystery man.

"Stune, what do you think?" asked Klage.

The frail man jumped and ran to the side of the emperor. "Sire, we don't have to judge them now," he said with a wave of his hand, his eyes glowing pink. His voice was softer and more timid than before. "Besides, we have that meeting to attend to."

Klage sighed, "Just throw them in the dungeon already," he uttered as he locked eyes with Tsuki. Something was off about his eyes, but Tsuki couldn't put her finger on it.

Stune laughed, triggering Tsuki to remember her dream the night before. But before she could investigate further, they were taken away.

Chapter Nineteen

In the Dungeon

THE NEXT THING Tsuki knew was that they were in one of the rattiest dungeons she had ever seen. There was no bed, just straw in one corner and a bucket in the other as a makeshift toilet. Tsuki had thought the guards were rude before, but when they opened the cell door, the guards threw Tsuki and her friends in and slammed the door.

"Ugh! Rude!" Tsuki yelled as the guards walked away laughing.

"Everyone alright?" Alistain asked with a huff.

Kiriuk stood up and rushed to the locked door of the cell. "Hey! Let us go!"

"Quiet you!" said a voice from the doorway leading to the cells. Through the doorway came Stune. He turned and shut the door behind him. "You just had to come to the capital now, didn't you?" Stune continued with confidence and venom that sent a chill down the spines of the group. He had a much different tone than in the throne room. He even had a different posture. He was carrying an air of power.

Takagi rushed the bars of the cell and spit back, "How dare you talk to us that way. You have no idea who we are, do you?"

Stune held his hand up as if he had heard enough. "I don't speak to those below me unless I have to. Now be quiet and listen well."

Tsuki was furious now. Not only were they attacked and detained for no reason, they were thrown in a cell and locked up like some sort of criminal. And now, this man had the audacity to talk to her royal advisor like that. She had had enough and was about to yell that man's ear off. But before she could even inhale to speak, the man started up again.

"Since you are Urufian, I will have him make you an example. That should start the war I'm wanting. And I will finally have everything I want." Stune smiled as he laughed maniacally while his purple eyes glowed pink. "Tomorrow at sunrise, you will be executed. Thus sparking the fight between our countries. Then I will have all the captured werewolves sent to the front lines to be slaughtered."

"What the hell do you have against werewolves?" Tsuki growled as she stood.

Alistain touched her shoulder, "Don't let him provoke you. He's just trying to make you justify our death."

Stune made a 'tut' as he crossed his arms. "A turncoat and a... half-breed? How utterly disgusting. Now I absolutely *have* to orchestrate your death; *things* like you should be dealt with swiftly," he scrunched his nose as he walked away, waving his hand in the air and talking about how he was going to throw up. He then opened the door and walked away, making a gagging noise.

Moments later, Tsuki was pacing the cell while Willianna was at the door, and everyone else was sitting on the straw. Two guards came through the door that Stune went through. They were talking amongst themselves. It was past supper time, and the group hadn't eaten anything since breakfast.

Tsuki was still furious at being treated like scum. But she was even more so that her friends were also being treated like that. She didn't know about the others but deeply understood what it felt like to be worthless.

That's when Kiriuk's stomach growled from hunger. It broke Tsuki's train of thought. She turned to look at Kiriuk.

Kiriuk looked embarrassed and upset. He got up from the straw and went to the bars of the cell. He started yelling at the guards, "Hey! Why haven't we gotten anything to eat? Do you Heltavins not eat? We are likely to starve before our execution!"

"Shhh!" hushed Willianna. She was still at the gate with her hands at the lock. She jabbed Kiriuk with her knee.

"Ow! what was… Oh!" Kiriuk shouted. "Sorry." He commented softer, covering his mouth.

Tsuki got curious and went beside Willianna to see what she was doing. As Tsuki got closer, she realized that Willianna was picking the lock to the cell.

"By the Moon Goddess, where did you stash that?" Tsuki whispered.

Willianna gave Tsuki a sneaky smile and continued her work on the lock. It didn't take long for her to open the door. Thankfully, the door was well-oiled, so it wasn't loud enough to open as the group snuck out of the cell and away from the guards at the door.

As the group approached a door out of the dungeon, Willianna turned around and put a finger to her lips to signal everyone to be quiet. She said quietly, "I saw the armory on our way to the dungeon. Follow me, and for goodness sake, be silent." She then opened the door slightly. After a few seconds, Willianna pushed the door open and slipped through; the rest of the group followed suit.

Sneaking through the castle, the group finally found the armory. Upon pushing the door open, the group found their confiscated weapons. One guard was in the room, sharpening his blade with his back turned to the group.

Takagi stepped silently forward from the back of the group and placed a hand on Willianna's shoulder to stop her from moving forward. He then took a deep breath, and with a swirl of his hands, a short chant under his breath, and a flick of a hand toward the opposed man, Takagi sent a magic spell flying toward the man in the armory.

The spell hit the man, who suddenly sat upright, then slowly slouched and went limp, leaning against the wall with his head bowed, his sword still in hand.

"What spell was that?" Alistain asked quietly.

"A sleep spell. I have several quick, minor spells ready to use at any time without my book," Takagi said with a proud smile at the group.

Kiriuk chuckled, "Yeah, big bro is awesome with magic. I saw many of his tricks while we were searching for Tsuki."

The group entered the armory and quickly grabbed their weapons and gear. Willianna and her slingshot, Takagi with his spell book, Kiriuk's spear, and Alistain's rapier. They each checked their equipment and readied themselves for a fight as Tsuki kept a lookout at the door. They knew it wouldn't be easy, but they had to get out of the capital and regroup.

As the group readied themselves, Tsuki, who was at the door, heard two guards pass by the room. She quickly shushed her friends and listened to the guards' conversation.

"Man, Advisor Stune is so harsh with everyone but the Emperor. He acts so weak and feeble when with the Imperial Majesty but is a demon with us," said one guard.

"I know, right? And the Emperor has been acting strangely and impulsively this last year. It's like a total turnaround from his usual self," sighed the other guard as they walked past the door.

Once they had moved far away from the room she and her friends were in, Tsuki turned to the others and mentioned the Emperor's eyes that she noticed in the throne room earlier. "This whole situation feels off. Like the emperor isn't in control of himself."

Takagi nodded, "I sensed a magic spell being activated while we were in the throne room. Maybe this advisor is putting thoughts in the Emperor's head to make him do what he wants."

"Like a puppet master?" Kiriuk asked.

"That would make sense." Alistain joined in.

Willianna put her hand out in front of her and said, "Then let's go find this Stune guy and give him a what for. Maybe even get the Emperor to see reason."

Everyone nodded and placed their hand on top of Willianna's.

"Right! Let's do this!" said Tsuki as she placed her hand on the top of the pile.

With that, the group sneaked around the castle searching for Stune, the advisor to the Heltavin Emperor. A stray guard here and there had to be knocked out, but with Takagi's magic, it was quick and easy. Once they finally found Stune, he was in the throne room with the Emperor, and the room was lined with guards.

The group waited for what seemed like forever for Stune to leave the Emperor's side, but he didn't budge. Suddenly, from behind them, Tsuki heard, "Found them! They are trying to get into the throne room!"

Tsuki looked back at the sound and saw three guards running at them. She made a split decision and bolted into the throne room. In desperation, she pointed at Emperor Klage and yelled, "As one royal to another, I will free you from his spell!"

Klage had a blank expression, eyes filled with a pink aura.

Stumbling over his words, Stune jumped and tried to cover himself, "S-stupid girl, what are you talking about? G-get them, now!" he said.

The next thing Tsuki knew, three guards were charging at her and clunking as they came from where she had entered. Tsuki ran and drop-kicked one of the guards, knocking him out and surprising the other guards attacking her. She grabbed the legs of one of the other guards, making him fall into his compatriot with a crash of armor. Tsuki got up from the ground and readied her stance to fight.

As her opponents clambered up, Tsuki looked around. Her friends were all fighting enemies and had nearly taken care of them. Takagi was trading spells with Stune, who was hiding behind the throne.

Kiriuk had changed into a wolf and was dancing around five guards, all trying to get at him. Willianna knocked guards out with her slingshot, and Alistain was in a heated sword fight with Klage.

Tsuki squared up to one of the guards, with more flooding into the room, and immediately socked him in the jaw so hard he stumbled backward and crumpled to the floor. The other stood wide-eyed and stared at Tsuki. She chuckled and took a step towards him. He was quick to turn tail and run.

As she finished her fight, Tsuki heard Stune say, “You insolent worm. Fine, I will do it myself!”

Tsuki turned to face the throne and saw Stune throwing a pink swirling spell at her. Even with her quick reflexes, she wouldn’t have gotten out of the way in time.

Suddenly, a flash of blue came in front of Tsuki, and was hit by the pink blast. Takagi had jumped in front of Tsuki and taken the opponent's spell full force.

Tsuki outstretched her arms and caught her friend as he was thrown back from the spell's force. She could feel a warm wetness seep into her hands and chest as Takagi started to bleed from his wound. Tsuki laid Takagi in her arms as she slowly went to the ground.

“Takagi!” Tsuki cried out, looking at the extent of the wound. It wasn’t too wide, but it was deep.

"Tsuki, I need you to listen to me. I need to tell you the truth before I pass out." Takagi said, his horse voice just above a whisper.

"What are you talking about?" Tsuki cried out as she started to panic.

"I am in love with you. I have been since we reunited, but I knew you only had love for Alistain, so I hid it." Takagi weakly vowed as a blood-soaked hand came to rest on Tsuki's cheek.

Tsuki shook her head. "Wh-why now? You can't! You can't do this!"

"Alistain dislikes my feelings for you because he thinks I will take you away from him. But I would never want that," Takagi continued. His voice got softer and softer as he got weaker and weaker. "I just want someone to love..." was all that Takagi said before passing out.

"That's what you get, you annoying blue twit," Stune cursed with a smirk.

Tsuki looked up at Stune, who had emerged from hiding behind the throne.

She then looked around; Will was shooting the last of her stones at the assailants who were slowly cornering her. She brought out her knife when she depleted her ammo. Kiriuk had several guards on top of him and were holding him down. He struggled and would nearly get up after throwing guards off him before more would topple him down. Alistain was trading blows with Klage, who was wielding a large sword. Most of the swings from Alistain were defensive, as Klage was stronger. In the blink of an eye, Alistain was knocked down and had Klage's sword at his throat.

"Face it, insolent girl. You've lost," Stune said haughtily.

Tsuki looked down at Takagi and closed her eyes. Had she lost? Was she and everyone she loved about to be killed?

Rage filled her entire being.

No. She wasn't just going to let the people who counted on her die. She wasn't going to let them or her country down.

Tsuki clenched her eyes and let the rage she felt consume her. "RRRAAAAAAAAHHHHH!" she screamed as she got up from Takagi's side. She then opened her eyes, and the color in them filled her eyes. The left one was completely silver, and the right fully blue. Her fangs had grown, and her hair and fur had puffed up.

She clenched her jaw when she locked eyes with Stune, who had his eyes wide and was chanting a defensive spell.

She stepped over Takagi's motionless form and started toward the puny Stune. She put a hand out to the side, and an orb of light appeared just as before and formed so easily from her hand. Tsuki slowly walked towards Stune, and as she did so, the orb got bigger and bigger. The orb reached two meters in diameter before Tsuki started running at Stune. It looked like a small moon.

Tsuki wildly screamed as she jumped and threw the orb at the gray-headed wizard. The orb met Stune's magical shield and pressed it back, but it did not break through.

Stune started to laugh maniacally when Foxy Brown ran into the room from the side and bit Stune's ankle. The surprise attack took Stune's concentration from his shield spell to kick Foxy Brown off his ankle. When he did so, his spell faltered and broke as the force of the orb pushed past it. Foxy Brown then ran to Kiriuk and started to growl at the guards on top of Kiriuk.

The orb then connected with Stune and exploded, knocking him and Tsuki, still in the air, in opposite directions from the explosion of magic. Tsuki flew across the room into Klage, and Stune was blasted into the wall behind the throne, knocking him out.

When Tsuki opened her eyes again, they were back to normal, and her rage had dissipated. She climbed off of Klage, whom she had landed on, and knocked on top of Alistain. When she turned to Klage, they locked eyes. Klage's eyes were the same color as Alistain's, a blood red. They were no longer pink like before.

"What happened? Who are you, and why do I have my sword drawn?" Klage said. His voice was still slightly monotone but did have some emotion in it.

"You were being mind-controlled by your advisor," Alistain commented with a grunt as he stood.

Klage looked around at Tsuki, then Stune, and then focused on Takagi. "Men, get yourselves to the healers and help those who need it." He then quickly walked over to Takagi and knelt down. He placed a hand over Takagi's badly wounded body, which was in a pool of blood.

"Divine powers that be, mend and weave. Heal this body and place my seal. Put back what was out of keel." Klage spoke as a magic circle appeared above Takagi. The circle was black and glowing as Klage repeated the same sentences. His red pendant was also glowing with a pulsating light.

The blood pooled around Takagi started to flow back into him, and the flesh that had been rent by the spell from Stune started to fix itself.

As the wound started to heal by Klage's magic, Takagi's chest started to move up and down as he returned to breathing. When the wound nearly healed, Tsuki knelt down at Takagi's side. Suddenly, Takagi's eyes opened, and he took a deep, gasping breath.

"Thank the Moon Goddess, you saved him!" Tsuki exclaimed as she grabbed Takagi's hand in joy.

"My father was a great healer and taught me some useful spells," Klage nodded as he finished the healing that needed to be done. "Sadly, it can't be cast multiple times in one day."

Chapter Twenty

Quest End

TAKAGI WAS BROUGHT to the castle's infirmary and was seen by the trained healers, greatly impressed by Klage's healing spell's work. Takagi was in and out of sleep for a few hours, Tsuki never leaving his side. When he finally regained consciousness, he saw Tsuki sitting beside him, talking with Alistain.

"Like I said, I don't know how to control how big it gets; it just kind of happens," Tsuki said.

Takagi gave Tsuki's hand a squeeze. She looked down to see he was awake. "Oh! He's awake!" Tsuki exclaimed.

"Oi idiot!" Alistain said as he smacked Tsuki's hand out of Takagi's. "What was that? Jumping in front of a spell you knew you couldn't block in time. You made her worry!"

Takagi sat up slightly and said with as much strength as possible, "It's not like you were doing anything useful."

"I was preoccupied by a man who wanted to cut my head off!" Alistain yelled back.

“Quit it!” Tsuki yelled angrily.

Both men stopped and looked at her, all the venom in their demeanor gone.

“We are a family! Why can’t we love each other without fighting?” Tsuki yelled at the two of them, a tear traveling down her cheek.

The two looked at each other and then looked away. “I love both of you. Takagi, I might not be sure if it’s romantic or familial love right now, but I do love you.” Tsuki said with a soft smile. “That won’t ever change. Plus, no one has ever told me I couldn’t love more than one person.”

Both men looked at each other again and burst out laughing. Takagi laughed through the pain left over from the healing process of his injury.

“What?” Tsuki asked innocently.

Alistain shook his head and said, “There’s the naive little pup I love.”

Tsuki realized what she had said and started to blush and become shy. “Shush! I’m not naive. I’m just not as quick-witted as you two.”

“And that’s okay. We still love you,” Takagi said fondly, smiling softly.

Tsuki and Alistain brought Takagi up to speed. He had been out for about three days. During those three days, Stune had been imprisoned for the rest of his life. Tsuki and Klage had agreed to sit down and talk peace for Urufu and Heltavin, and Klage had retracted all the evil decrees he had made under Stune's spell.

Klage didn't remember much of the year and a half that Stune controlled him. He had hazy memories of discussions in the throne room dominated by Stune. After interrogating Stune for a few hours, he revealed that he had slipped some hallucinogens into Klage's food. Once his mind was weakened, Stune used a mind-control spell lasting several days. Stune would then repeat this cycle until he got caught and imprisoned.

"And ya know, Willianna has been spending much time with Klage." Tsuki said off-handedly with a crooked grin.

"Well, by the looks of it, you don't even need a royal advisor." Takagi said with a chuckle.

"Don't even joke about that! I would be lost with all this diplomatic stuff. Sure, put a monster in front of me, and I can deal with it. But put me in front of a bunch of nobles? I will do everything wrong on my own," Tsuki spoke defiantly as she crossed her arms.

After Tsuki had spoken on the matter, Willianna, Kiriuk, and Klage walked into the infirmary and over to where Takagi's bed with Foxy Brown trailing behind them.

"Looks like the magic man is up," Willianna mentioned smugly.

"Big bro!" Kiriuk yelled as he ran up to Takagi's bed and hugged him tightly.

"Ouch!" Takagi cried out.

Tsuki slapped Kiriuk on the back of the head and told Kiriuk to not hug so tightly as it hurt his compatriot.

Once Kiriuk was done with his overly dramatic spiel about how Takagi was so brave and how he was so proud to have him as a big brother, Klage approached the group.

Takagi turned to Klage and placed his hand on his chest. "Thank you, your Imperial Majesty. You saved my life! I am forever in your debt."

Klage shook his head. "It is I who should be thanking you and your friends. You defeated that rat Stune and broke his spell on me. Who knows what he would have done if you hadn't stopped him. Healing you was my duty as one with power and a man who knows right from wrong."

"I can tell you are a good man, Klage." Tsuki said almost unconsciously. "Good leaders know when to take care of those around them."

"And good leaders protect those around them," Klage nodded. "Once you feel up to it, wizard, we will talk peace."

Suddenly, a man who looked to be a messenger ran into the infirmary. "His Imperial Majesty, Imperial Majesty! Word has reached us that your younger brother has been taken by pirates who sailed south of the continent." said the out-of-breath messenger.

"My brother? Foolish boy, I told him not to go to the coast," Klage said, shaking his head in dismay.

As curious as a cat, Tsuki asked, "Why did you not want him to go to the coast?"

Klage sighed and turned to Tsuki. "Pirates have been plaguing our southern coast, wrecking villages and taking people. They all bear the same flag, so it must be a fleet. They are also different from other sailors because they have some sort of water serpents that they ride when they attack."

Tsuki nodded as she listened. "Well…" she started to say.

Alistain put a hand on her shoulder. "We will follow your lead."

"Klage, if you want, we could go and investigate," Tsuki said slightly tentatively.

Klage looked shocked. "You would do that? Even though our countries are enemies? And you don't even know my brother."

"A good leader knows when to help others." Tsuki smiled. "Besides, you have a big enough mess after all that's happened with Stune. We can go get your brother back."

After thinking briefly, Klage shook his head and said, "Thank you. I am forever indebted to you, Tsuki."

Tsuki, determined to help those in need, stuck a hand out to Klage.

Klage took her hand and breathed deeply, “Bring my brother home.

The End

Author's Note

Firstly, thank you for reading my book. This is my first publication and means the world to me. I started writing around the age of twelve. I was and am an avid reader, and the idea of making your own world and characters through writing fascinated me. And thus, I came up with a character. Her name was Kusay, who I later renamed Tsuki. She was courageous and brave, with powers to change the world. I hope Tsuki can teach lessons about strength and love despite everything being against you. And I hope that these lessons will be heard.

www.ingramcontent.com/pod-product-compliance
Lightning Source LLC
Chambersburg PA
CBHW030559310726
48979CB00003B/502

* 9 7 9 8 9 8 8 6 0 4 0 6 8 *